The Quondam Lover
and Other Stories
from the Wasteland

The Quondam Lover and Other Stories from the Wasteland

James Whitmer

THE QUONDAM LOVER AND OTHER
STORIES FROM THE WASTELAND

iUniverse books may be ordered through booksellers or by contacting:

iUniverse
1663 Liberty Drive
Bloomington, IN 47403
www.iuniverse.com
844-349-9409

ISBN: 978-1-6632-3062-1 (sc)
ISBN: 978-1-6632-3063-8 (e)

Library of Congress Control Number: 2021921544

Print information available on the last page.

iUniverse rev. date: 10/27/2021

"This book is dedicated to Jessica and Lindsey."

Contents

Blue Windows

Chapter 1

"What ya' got, Sarge?" Maysmith asked.

That would be Detective John Maysmith, a hardened veteran of Robbery-Homicide who had been investigating mayhem and malevolence in the Windy City for over 25 years.

What did I have? ShotSpotter indicated that there were several gunshots fired on the block where we now found ourselves conducting a neighborhood. But what did I have? Just a whole lot of nothing.

"I think we'll call it a night, boys," I said, as Maysmith and the other detectives, some slump-shouldered, others simply stressed out from the long day typified by shooting after shooting in the City with Big Shoulders, gathered around my squad car.

"Hit it hard again in the morning then, Sarge?" asked Maysmith.

"Yeah, bright and early, girls. See you in the squad area," I said, tipping the hat which I did not have on my head and then opening the door to my squad car.

Within a matter of minutes I was alone in the dimly lit street, sitting in my squad car and just dotting some *i*'s and crossing some *t*'s on the canvass report of the evening's activities. By the way, I am Detective Sergeant James Price and I head a unit in Robbery-Homicide assigned to the district where the recent shots were fired.

As I packed up, getting ready to vacate the area, a light flickered on in a window across the street from where I was parked. I had knocked on that door earlier in the evening but there had been no response. Now it appeared as if someone was at home. I looked at my watch, almost midnight. I had pulled another 24-hour shift and I was just plain exhausted but there was something about the window from where the light was coming. I remembered that an oval-shaped piece of glass was hung over it from the inside and it was tinted an odd-looking blue color, almost indigo, and as blue as the gumballs on my squad car. Whatever for I could only imagine but now, however, it was somehow drawing me toward it. Oh, what the hell, knocking on one more door in the middle of the night wouldn't kill me.

So I knocked on the door, announcing police business. It was an old door that severely needed painting and as I knocked with my blackjack I noticed that some paint chips fell off and floated to the ground. The door then slowly opened but was held back by a thick chain lock.

"Yes," a soft voice said.

"Police business, ma'am," I said, holding up my detective's shield.

"How do I know it's real?" The soft voice again.

Good question. I thought for a moment.

"Well, if you look out of your window, ma'am, you will see my squad car. I'll just go over and activate the lights and siren for you," I said. "I think that will suffice."

The door slowly closed without her saying a word, as I walked toward my squad car but before I reached it she was opening the door again.

"Please, come in, officer," she said.

Chapter 2

It was a small apartment, just four rooms, a bathroom, a kitchen, a small bedroom located behind the kitchen and a larger room, a catchall of sorts, that served as another bedroom and whatever else anyone would want it to be. The apartment was dimly lit by a flickering lamp that was standing on a small coffee table in the corner of the large room. In the ambient light I made out two figures, an old woman and a young woman, the latter having opened the door and invited me inside.

"Sorry to inconvenience you, ma'am," I said to the younger woman. "But there were shots fired in the neighborhood recently and I just wanted to see if you had heard anything."

"Please, have a seat, Detective," the younger woman said, indicating a worn-out couch of an ugly green color. "It is Detective, isn't it?"

"Yes, ma'am, Detective Price, James Price," I said as I reached for my shield.

"No need for that, Detective," she said. "Please, sit. Now then, you were saying that shots were fired."

The older woman remained in the kitchen at a table that appeared to be as old as she was. The younger woman, seated across from me with her knees tightly clamped together and her hands neatly folded, leaned slightly forward into the ambient light. I could now see that she was in her late 20's or thereabouts. Her long, black hair reached almost to her waist. Her skin was a deep olive color, reminding me of sun-drenched beaches, and her eyes were a dark emerald green. She had an exotic look about her that made me envision gypsy caravans careening along winding mountain roads in the dead of night. Something about her was strangely forbidding yet, at the same time, alluring. Her voice was mellow and soft, as if she had never uttered a harsh word in her life.

"Yes, we pinpointed the shots fired to this area," I said.

"Well, we just arrived home a short time ago. So it seems we have missed out on all the excitement. I'm sorry that we can't be of any help to you," she said, as she exchanged glances with the ancient doyen who stiffly sat at the kitchen table, her hands splayed across the table as if she were at a séance and willing the table to rise. I got up to politely excuse myself and leave. The young woman followed suit, extending her small hand to me.

"Perhaps another time, Detective," she said.

"Another time?"

"Yes, it seems that Vadoma has intuited that you would like your fortune read," she said, indicating the old woman. "We are gypsies, you know."

"Vadoma?"

"Yes, she is my grandmother and her name means *to know*. She reads fortunes and councils people," she said.

I looked at the old woman, whose lower lip was slightly drooping and exposing what I believed to be an attempt at a smile.

"And I am Esmeralda. My name is the Portuguese version of emerald. I was named Esmeralda because of my eye color," she said.

"Well, perhaps I can have my fortune read," I said. "But I …"

Esmeralda interrupted me with a slight wave of her hand. She then approached Vadoma and leaned close to her, as Vadoma whispered something into her ear. She then came back to where I was standing.

"Vadoma said tomorrow evening will be fine," she said.

"Tomorrow, I have to …"

Another slight hand wave from Esmeralda cut me off.

"She says that she will tell you about the blue window tomorrow, as well, as she has ascertained that it is somewhat on your mind."

I was taken aback by such clairvoyance and I could not formulate a logical response. Possibly I had been looking at the oval-shaped piece of blue glass, which the old woman referred to as a window, in such a way that she had imagined that I was curious about its origin. Those thoughts were soon dismissed from my mind, as the door was slowly opened by Esmeralda, after which she politely squeezed my hand.

"Until tomorrow, Detective," she said. "Shall we say 7:00 p.m.?"

Chapter 3

It had been another long day and the boys wanted to stop and have a nightcap before heading home.

"You're coming, right, Sarge?" asked Detective Maysmith.

"Sorry, ladies, but I'm getting my fortune read tonight," I said.

"So you finally got a date with that redhead from Closed Section," Maysmith laughed.

A date with Clara from Closed Section would certainly be appealing but, on the other hand, there was something about Esmeralda that seemed to be popping in and out of my mind most of the day. Sure, I was stopping by to get my fortune read by a woman who was older than dirt but that was really only a pretext for having another encounter with the mysterious, yet lovely, Esmeralda.

"Nah, maybe next week. Gotta' go," I said.

"Hit it hard in the morning again, Sarge?" asked Maysmith.

I simply nodded but I really wasn't listening. I was thinking of deep emerald eyes and glistening long black hair. It didn't take long to get there as I was in the neighborhood. She was waiting at the door when I arrived, the flickering light from inside of the small apartment casting an eerie glow onto the blue window.

"Vadoma is excited that you have agreed to come," she said. "But, please, be patient. She does not speak English and I must interpret."

Esmeralda was wearing a long velvet dress with a thick black belt with a silver buckle. Her eyes were shaded with a tinge of green slightly lighter than her twinkling emerald eyes. Her lips were colored a deep scarlet and her long black hair reached almost to her waist. She wore golden hoop earrings the size of quarters in each ear that seductively danced as she spoke.

"Please, be seated," Esmeralda said.

I took my appointed place opposite the ancient crone at the kitchen table. It appeared as if she had not eaten a decent meal in sometime. Her hands were bony and as wrinkled as the surface of the moon, yet there was a glimmer of laughter appearing to birth itself from her close-set eyes, the color of which could only be described as black as old coal.

"Relax, Detective. She likes you," said Esmeralda.

"Why?" I simply inquired.

"Because you were polite to me. Because you were concerned about our safety. Because you are curious about her blue window. Now then, shall we begin? I will act as interpreter," she said.

She then lit two small blue candles, which she placed on the table. Vadoma then outstretched her hands toward me, face up, her eyes somewhat gleaming, indicating to me that I should reciprocate and lay my hands upon hers.

"Please, James, lay your hands upon hers," said Esmeralda, who was sitting next to Vadoma, her long hair glistening in the soft ambient light from the flickering candles.

So I did. The old woman's hands were rough and dry, feeling to me as if they had known severe pain and grief throughout her many years. As she gently moved them back and forth over my hands, massaging my palms with cracked and wrinkled fingers, I felt a pulse of energy beginning to flow into me. It was not painful but it felt as if I needed to squeeze her hands tightly and so I did. I then attempted to look into her eyes but they were closed. The old woman then whispered something to Esmeralda in what I imagined was her native gypsy tongue.

"Do you dream of roses, James?" Esmeralda asked.

"Roses?" I asked.

"Yes, Vadoma senses that you dream of roses because the single rose is a symbol for perfection. Are you striving for perfection in your work, James? Perhaps you are striving for perfection in your life."

"My mother's name was Rosemarie but she has been dead for quite a long time and I really don't dream about her," I said.

Vadoma resumed massaging my palms, as an unexplained easy feeling came over me. I felt the stress of the day gradually leaving me. I felt receptive to her curious machinations. Then she again was whispering something into Esmeralda's ear.

"What language is that?" I asked.

"It is Romani, James. As I told you, we are gypsies. We are from Macedonia. Now then, Vadoma wants to know if you were to give me a rose, what color would it be and how many petals would it have?"

I looked deeply into Esmeralda's emerald eyes, losing myself in unnamed possibilities. Of course, as I gazed into those magnificent portals of unsolved love the color green ruled my world but who had ever heard of a green rose? Then for some odd reason, for which I simply had no explanation, other than I was possibly thinking of the blue window, I blurted out the color blue followed by eight petals. With that being said the ancient crone slowly removed her hands from mine and then leaned closer to Esmeralda, whispering something in Romani into her ear.

"She is tired now, James," Esmeralda said.

"But we haven't discussed the blue window," I said, indicating the oval-shaped blue piece of glass that hung over the front window of their apartment.

"Next time, James, because there will be a next time. Vadoma is extremely fond of you and so am I. Now I must help her into bed. She is tired. I will only be a moment."

I sat alone in the room, my eyes affixed on the oval-shaped blue glass, wondering what deep meaning, if any, it portended. It reminded me of a porthole on a ship crossing the ocean or the view from a bungalow on some secluded island facing the blue-green sea. In a few moments Esmeralda was back and we were seated next to each other on the ugly green couch in the large room.

"I have to ask you, Esmeralda, how do you survive? How do you make ends meet? I hope I am not being impertinent to ask but …"

She interrupted me, placing her slender finger on my lips.

"James, it is a proper question. I feel that you are concerned for us," she said.

I was concerned. Two, more or less, vulnerable women living in a mixed-use neighborhood on the near southside of Chicago where only the day before shots had been fired, yes, I was concerned for their safety.

"Vadoma ekes out a meager existence telling fortunes. As for me, I am a graduate student at the University of Chicago studying Race, Class and Gender issues and focusing on our culture, Romani people. You know, we have been maligned and persecuted over the centuries. I am not concerned with money, James. I am concerned with telling the world of how my people have been victimized over the years. I do, however, receive a meager stipend from the university for the research I am conducting and we seem to make do with what we have," she said.

"Well, I am certainly going to pay Vadoma for the session," I said, reaching into my pocket.

"Please, James, that is not necessary. She is protective of me and she likes you," said Esmeralda. "Now about the color of the rose you chose, blue, wasn't it?"

I removed my hand from my pocket, remembering what I had told the old woman.

"Yes, perhaps, I was focused on her blue window when I made my choice."

"Blue, James, is symbolic of the impossible. That is what Romani people believe and the number of petals that you chose, eight, wasn't it?"

"Yes."

"Romani people believe that the eight-petalled rose signifies regeneration."

"Regeneration? Regeneration of what?" I asked, somewhat confused.

"That, James, along with the concept of impossibilities, we will discuss next time. Perhaps you could come for dinner tomorrow evening, hmm?"

"And discuss her blue window, as well?" I asked.

"Among other things, yes."

Chapter 4

As the door slowly opened, I saw that she was wearing an evening gown of the purest white that was trimmed in gold lace. Her jet black hair caressed her shoulders like a lost lover, inviting me to be that lost lover. Her hoop earrings were not golden as before but were a bright silver and were the size of silver dollars. Her emerald eyes sparkled as always and drew me into her realm of mystique. Who was she? Why did she affect me so intensely?

"I have been anxious. I wasn't sure you would come," she said, reaching out for my hand. "I am so relieved that you are here."

I took her gentle hand in mine. Her long and slender fingers caressed my hand as if she would do anything for love.

"Have you been thinking of me, James?" she asked, as she led me into the room with the green couch.

We were now seated next to each other, her lips close to mine but not touching. For some uncanny reason I could not speak and then her delicate fragrance was upon me, entrapping my emotions in a cloudy illusion of what I imagined love should be.

"James, is loving me impossible?" she asked in a somewhat frantic voice, an unadorned frown on her upturned face.

"Wake up, Sarge. Are you okay?" asked Maysmith.

He was shaking me by my shoulders. I lifted my head from my desk, which was cluttered with a spattering of police reports, some finished, some unfinished. I began rubbing the dust out of my eyes as Maysmith's voice descended upon me again like a rambling waterfall.

"Are you with us, Sarge? Are you okay?"

Gathering my senses, I glanced at my watch. I was going to be late.

Chapter 5

As before, she was waiting for me at the door, a gentle smile on her face.

"I'm sorry that I am late," I said. "But I ..."

Her slender finger was instantly upon my lips. Her emerald eyes were dancing the adagio as she gently took my hand and led me inside.

"James, you are in police work. We understand that your hours, shall we say, are commonly irregular."

"That sums it up nicely," I said.

"Now first we shall eat dinner. Vadoma has prepared her favorite dish for you from the old country and then we will discuss colored roses and impossibilities, hmm," she said in a soft voice.

Vadoma was busy stirring something in a charred pot that was simmering on the small stove. She looked up at me and smiled, her eyes as dark as the evening before. The smell of garlic, if not overpowering, was surely biting.

"It is like a stew, James. She has included chicken this time with the potatoes, paprika and bell peppers. For desert, she has made a type of pudding called *pirogo*. It contains eggs and raisins, and she has added a walnut or two mixed in with the egg noodles. It is quite tasty," Esmeralda said. "I think she is ready, James. Shall we?"

The meal was tasty. It was also spicy as hell but I imagined that was simply the Romani way. It was topped off with a glass or two of a red gypsy wine that when spilled on my napkin left a deep scarlet stain. The old woman, however, did not talk during the meal, nor did she eat or drink anything. She only smiled at me with her ancient hands neatly folded, yet her dark eyes never wavered from their severe tenor. They simply appeared as small dark orbs adrift in a sea of mysticism and when the meal was finished and the table was cleared, she again placed her upturned gnarled and withered hands onto the table in front of me, inviting me to do the same.

I did so as before and again soon felt a small surge of energy entering into them. Possibly, it was only my imagination but before I could dwell on that curiosity, she was whispering in Esmeralda's ear.

"She said that last time you chose the blue rose and that, James, is symbolic of the impossible. She wants to know what in your life you consider impossible."

Impossible? A hundred things entered my mind at the same time. I simply was not skilled at answering open-ended questions. I was, however, inordinately skilled at asking them and so I was somewhat tongue-tied in providing a response to her question.

"Well, many things in my life are impossible," I said. "It is difficult for me to put my finger on any particular one."

"So you are saying that it is impossible to define the impossibilities in your life, James?" asked Esmeralda, an intriguing grin on her face.

"Well, I …"

Before I could answer further, the old woman was whispering into Esmeralda's ear again.

"She wants to know about love, James. Is love impossible for you? She is asking the question because you have chosen an eight-petalled rose which signifies regeneration. You see, James, if you put the two concepts together, possibly you can renew love in some respect. She simply wants to know if you have ever been in love, James."

The old woman's coarse and uneven hands were gently massaging mine as Esmeralda spoke. Her dark eyes remained stillborn.

"I am 40-years old and I have known many women but, frankly, I have never been in love," I bluntly said.

The words came out of my mouth as if fired from a cannon during the *1812 Overture*. I wanted to suck them back in and stamp them out, especially the part about many women, but once a can of worms is opened, well, it rarely can be resealed. So I just sheepishly sat there feeling considerably embarrassed, as the ancient crone continued her whispering, her eyes remaining shut.

"She said that is good, James. She said that you are an honest person and she said that you will fall in love soon," said Esmeralda. "But now she is tired and I will take her to bed."

Chapter 6

We were back seated on the green couch.

"She did not speak of her blue window," I said.

"Of what would you rather speak, James, of love or of a blue window?" she asked.

Her hair was drifting toward me as she leaned closer and whispered in my ear. I wanted to reach out and live there, to dwell there for eternity. Her slender finger was upon my lips, running up and down as if on a string. She smelled of fragrant white gardenias mixed with rose water.

"Love, James, do you desire to be in love?" she whispered. "Vadoma believes that is what is missing in your life. You need to be regenerated, as signified by the eight-petalled rose with which you have identified."

I did want to be in love. But how could I tell her?

"Say nothing, James. Just show me," she whispered.

And so I did.

Chapter 7

When I arrived on the scene the paramedics had already departed. The crime scene tape that stretched across the entrance to the apartment restricted onlookers from entering the area, yet several stragglers remained gawking at the carnage. The blue oval-shaped piece of glass was completely shattered, shards of glass littering the ground outside and the floor within. As I deftly made my way through the crime scene, I encountered Detective Maysmith scribbling something in his notepad.

"Got here as soon as we could, Sarge," he said. "It was a 911 call but it came in rather late. We checked everything inside. It doesn't look like a burglary. Possibly a drive-by gone wrong. Front window was shattered to pieces from several rounds. Looks like a 9mm, maybe."

"The paramedics?" I frantically asked.

"Took an old woman from inside. Shot several times. Doesn't look good."

My heart sank to the lowest depths of my soul, as I summoned the courage to ask the next question.

"Anyone else inside?" I asked.

"Nope, just the old woman. She was conscious when we found her but she was speaking in a foreign language. Couldn't understand a damn thing she said. Queer, ain't it, an old woman like that living all alone in a neighborhood like this and not being able to speak English?"

"Where did they take her?" I asked.

"Hospital at the university," said Maysmith. "We're gonna' be here a while longer. Why don't you take a run over there? Maybe you can make out what she was saying. She was trying to tell us something, Sarge, that's for sure, but it just sounded like gibberish to me," said Maysmith.

"Right," I said, as I reached down and picked up a shard of the splintered blue glass and gently tucked it into my pocket.

Chapter 8

"Please, Detective, she should not be disturbed," the nurse said. "She's resting quietly now."

She was dressed in all white as if she were attempting to define the term antiseptic. She was about my age, judging from the wrinkles that were just beginning to emerge from the corners of her eyes. Her nametag pinned to her smock read Emily, a typical name for nurses. I then peeked through the open door and saw Vadoma strapped to a plethora of medical tubes and IV's. She appeared as if she was being attacked by an octopus.

"She's been mumbling since she was brought in here, Detective, but no one can understand what she is saying, except for maybe a few words in broken English," Emily said.

"She's a gypsy," I said. "She is speaking in Romani, their native language."

"Do you speak it?" asked Emily.

"Yes," I lied, needing to get close to the old woman and, hopefully, find out what had happened.

"Well, a moment or two won't make a difference at this point," she said.

In an instant I was standing next to the hospital bed, attempting to not entangle myself in all of the tubing that connected Vadoma to life support.

"She's been shot several times," said Emily. "None of the shots appear to be life-threatening but with her old age, and we really don't know if she has any pre-existing medical conditions, well, the doctors are presently weighing the odds of whether she will make it out of surgery if they pursue that option."

As I leaned closer I could hear the labored breathing of Vadoma. Then it was as if a light switch had suddenly been turned on and her eyes opened and in broken English she uttered my name – *James*. I grasped her hand, the one that did not have an IV attached to it. I squeezed it gently and leaned closer to her. Her eyes, as black as a Moscow midnight in December, appeared to be beckoning me closer. My ear was now upon her dry and chafed lips. In her dying breath she whispered two words to me - *Esmeralda* and *Bitola*. With that the heart monitor flatlined, yet the respirator continued to pump into a lost soul. Her hand became colder but I gently opened it up and from my pocket I tenderly placed into it the last vestige of whom she really was in life.

Chapter 9

"Macedonia? Why in God's name are you going to Macedonia?" asked Maysmith.

"North Macedonia," I said. "They changed the name a while back."

"Okay," said Maysmith. "I give."

"I think someone took her to Bitola. It's a town over there."

"Took who?"

"The young woman who lived with the old woman who just died."

"Oh, yeah, getting your fortune read, I remember now but is there something you're not telling me, Sarge?"

"I'm going to get her and bring her back if that's what you mean."

"Back from what?"

"She was forcibly taken, I'm sure of it," I said. "And I'm going to go and get her, damn it. I'm taking a leave of absence to do it."

"For how long for Chrissakes?"

"As long as it takes."

"Sarge, this ain't like in the movies. It's a foreign country. You don't know the language. You don't know the landscape. You can't do this by yourself," Maysmith said.

"I know. That's why I'm taking my best friend with me," I said.

"Now, Sarge, c'mon."

"Get your sorry ass down to Human Resources and put in the proper paperwork. We're leaving in the morning. I've already got the plane tickets."

"But what about Shirley?"

"Does she breathe fire when she orgasms?"

"Well, not exactly but …"

"Does she scream like a varsity cheerleader doing somersaults when you climax?"

"Not really but …"

"Does she make your muscles turn to hot jelly when she kisses you?"

"Well, kind of but not always and …"

"And that hornet's nest she calls a hairdo, what's with that?"

"Well, I've been trying to get her to …"

"Are you in love with her?"

"Well, no, I …"

"Exactly. So, damnit, I'm in love with Esmeralda. Now get home and start packing. We're leaving tomorrow."

Chapter 10

I had run down the landlord who rented the apartment where they had lived. I found out that their last name was Ibrahimi, a common Macedonian name equivalent to the American last name Smith. From the university I had found her adviser and had explained the situation to her in no uncertain terms. She was more than helpful, reviewing Esmeralda's background with me which was on file with the university. I was able to get a photograph of her but not of the old woman, who was only listed in her file as her grandmother and next of kin. I had also learned that Esmeralda had been born in Bitola, which is now located in present day North Macedonia, and that she had attended school there. I had written down a few contacts from Bitola she had listed on her application but that was almost three years ago and at this point in time I did not know if they were part of the problem or part of the solution as to what had happened to Esmeralda.

As the plane was about to land in Skopje, Maysmith was stirring from a long sleep. I had not slept much during the flight, just catching snippets of a cat nap here and there, mostly just trying to formulate a game plan as to what to do when we finally got to Bitola, which is just over a two hour drive from Skopje. Rubbing the sleep from his eyes, Maysmith looked at me, and never one to shy away from words he got right to the point.

"Needle in a haystack, Sarge, you know that don't you?"

I did know that. I also knew that if I didn't at least try to find her that my life would be meaningless.

"We have a chance but we have to find her first."

"And what is that chance?"

"Well, there is no American Consulate there, in Bitola, but there is a place where we can take her if we find her. It's called the American Corner Bitola. There are several other foreign consulates in the area. It should be a safe location."

"A corner what?"

"It's kind of like a consulate. It's actually a partnership between the Public Affairs Office of the U.S. Embassy located in Skopje, the capital, and the Ministry of Culture of North Macedonia. If we can get her there then we can arrange with the U.S. Embassy in Skopje for safe travel back to the United States for her."

"Do you know that for a fact or are you just guessing?"

I knew one thing for a fact. I was going to get her there by hook or by crook.

"It's a fact," I lied. "Now get focused. We'll be deplaning in a few minutes."

"Shot in the dark, Sarge. Damn needle in a haystack," said Maysmith.

Unfortunately, Detective John Maysmith was usually right.

Chapter 11

One Year Later

"Shot in the dark, Sarge," said Maysmith. "Damn needle in a haystack."

He was shaking me by the shoulders, the fog in my head as thick as week-old soup. Then I felt a cold splash of water assault the back of my head. I picked my crushed face up from the bar, something brown and soupy dripping from my chin, and my eyes encrusted with whatever accumulates on the surface of a cop bar after several hours of sitting there and drinking cheap bourbon.

"Sarge, it's been almost six months since we got back. Time to come back to the force and rejoin the human race. You did what you could. It's over now," said Maysmith, his arms now under mine as he lifted me up from the bar stool.

I wasn't thinking straight. Actually, I wasn't thinking at all but one thing was true, Detective John Maysmith was usually right. So as he propped me up and I gained my sea legs I began to focus on what he had just said – rejoin the human race.

"I'm taking you home, Sarge, and I'm going to clean you up. Then you're going to get a good night's sleep."

I looked into his eyes and nodded.

"And then you're coming back but before all that happens you're going to have a nice little chit-chat with Doris," he said.

"The police psychologist?" I managed to blurt out in between the dry coughs and nasal congestion.

"Exactly."

Detective John Maysmith was usually right about things.

Chapter 12

Doris was everything a female police psychologist would look like, with a frumpy hairdo that resembled a bird's nest, no make-up to speak of, eyes that squinted with every question she asked, a face that could only be described as the spitting image of the bottom of a hamster cage and of course, the obligatory, dull brown flat-bottomed shoes, the kind catholic grammar school teachers wear. As far as her personality, it was rather easy to describe because she simply didn't have one.

"Well, Detective Price, shall we get started?" she asked, pencil in hand, and with a stare that could freeze hot cat piss in mid-air at midnight in an alley on a steamy August evening.

"Cut the bullshit, Doris. You know my name. I've been in here enough," I said.

She rolled her eyes at me as if they were in a pinball machine.

"Okay, James, have it your way but this is going to be a professional evaluation of your fitness to return to duty, not some little chit-chat with tea and crumpets. Is that understood? I'm not a marriage counselor or a motivational coach."

A chit-chat, isn't that how Maysmith had described it? Well, okay, have it her way.

"Of course, Doris, now where do you want to start?"

"Where do you want to start?" she retorted, a smarmy expression on her face, as if she held a winning hand at blackjack.

Where did I want to start? Well, how about with my nightmares? That might be a good start.

"I'm having trouble sleeping," I said.

"Nightmares?" she asked.

"I guess you could call it that," I said.

Her office was cluttered and that was being diplomatic. I was having trouble seeing her face, which was shielded by a stack of papers and reports piled on top of her desk like the summit of Mount Kilimanjaro and that was littered with several half-filled coffee cups. Several more Styrofoam cups loaded with colored markers and pens appeared as sentinels on picket line duty.

"Well, tell me about them," she said. "Your nightmares."

I took a deep breath, really dreading to embrace what happens to me on a nightly basis.

"They are always the same. It's an eight-petaled blue rose that is most prominent. I reach out to touch its petals and then it wilts and turns an ugly black color, and then all turns dark. A deep and shadowy feeling of despair overpowers me and then I wake up sweating and despondent. Returning to sleep is impossible and I just spend the remainder of the night in a depressed and confused fog," I said.

"Is a woman involved?" she asked.

"Her name is Esmeralda and she is from Macedonia. She disappeared and I spent the last year trying to find her."

"And that's where you were during your leave of absence, in Macedonia trying to find her?" she asked.

"Six months in North Macedonia, yes. So you spoke with Detective Maysmith?"

"Well, he is the person who set up this appointment," she said.

"Yes, I was in and out of every pathetic run-down kiosk, hovel, and cheap hostel in that damn land-locked backward country."

"The rose, why are you dreaming about a rose? Why is it on your mind, James?" she then asked, abruptly switching gears.

"Esmeralda's grandmother was a fortune teller. They are gypsies and she read my fortune and somehow she arrived at a blue eight-petalled rose to describe my inner being and whom I really am."

"But you are dreaming, ultimately, of a black rose. Is any other color prominent in your mind?"

"Green. Esmeralda's eyes are a profound emerald green. I wish to hell I could dream about them but it's that damn black rose that is tormenting me."

"Well, James, green is typically associated with vegetation and growth but the color green can also be associated with death and lividness. Therefore, the color green is the connecting link between black, which signifies death and decomposition, and the color red, which signifies blood and life."

"Are you telling me that she is most likely dead?" I asked.

"I'm not telling you anything, James. I am just pointing out the possibilities. It is for you to decide the outcome. It is for you to get to the next step. Perhaps, recognizing that she is, in fact, dead may terminate your nightmares and lead you to recovery. You do want to recover, don't you, James?" she asked.

Recover from what? Lost love and come to grips with that finality?

"James, are you still with me?"

I wasn't hearing what she was saying, as the wilted black rose seeped into the crevices of my brain where memories are stored and the effervescent emerald eyes of Esmeralda faded into bleak nothingness, hidden within the fog of lost love.

Chapter 13

Somehow I had managed to convince Doris that I was fit for duty, so I was reinstated as an active duty detective. I think that Maysmith had a little to do with it, considering that Shirley, his girlfriend, and Doris are sisters but he never said as much and neither did Doris. Maysmith had also worked wonders in cleaning me up and keeping me straight. The nightmares, however, still persisted but we talked about them routinely, Maysmith and myself, and that seemed to diminish my pent-up anxiety to some extent.

"You haven't said much tonight," I said to Maysmith, who was seated across from me in a small booth in the rear of *Paulie's*, a cop bar with absolutely no atmosphere, bad-looking waitresses, but cheap booze.

We both, however, knew that it was the cheap booze that packed the place almost every night.

"I may have something," he said, as he slowly sipped his whiskey, straight up. "I just don't want to get you revved up over nothing."

If Maysmith was anything, he was thoroughly cautious. I read it in his eyes. I read it in his uncommon sullenness at the moment that did not fit his personality. Something was on his mind and bothering him but he was holding it back, as if to divulge it could lead to another dead end and diminish any future hopes of my finding her.

"Spit it out," I said. "I'm tired of talking in circles about my nightmares."

His eyes lit up like sparks from dormant coals onto which someone had blown their breath.

"I've been talking with the cold case boys, the ones who have the ticket on Vadoma's murder," he said straight-faced.

"Didn't we already gumshoe the hell out of that mess?"

"Right but something was bothering me, something about the glass," he said.

"You mean her blue window that was shattered into a thousand pieces?"

"Not necessarily a window, remember? It was just an oval-shaped piece of blue glass but you are right," he said. "Seems they just did a cursory examination of the shards and really came up with nothing important."

"So?"

"So I checked out a few of the shards, packaged them up, and sent them to Dawkins at the FBI Lab in Quantico."

"Dawkins?"

"Agent Dawkins, a guy I met when I went through the FBI National Academy. He works in the lab back there."

"And?"

"Well, I had them attempt to match the individual shards against a database they keep on file relative to glass found at crime scenes."

"Okay, I follow you so far," I said.

Maysmith took another hit from his whiskey tumbler and then pulled out a small notepad from his coat pocket.

"They did a chemical analysis of the stuff and at least some of it comes from a Greek island, Naxos. It's in the Aegean Sea," he said.

"Makes sense. Greece and Macedonia are like kissing cousins as far as countries go."

"Right and Vadoma was from Macedonia," Maysmith said.

"Okay, so where does that leave us?"

"Well, here's the kicker, Sarge. They were able to match some of the shards to shards in their database from another homicide. The guy's doing time in a federal joint, Sandstone in Minnesota," he said. "And he's Macedonian. Might be a connect there. Might be an opportunity."

"Sandstone, been there once years ago, a case I was working with the *G*," I said. "But that's a low security institution."

"Yeah, he's doing time up there on interstate truck thefts but he is still linked to the unsolved homicide, which took place in Gary, Indiana. Lots of Macedonians living in Gary, Sarge. That's in our backyard. It's worth a try, partner," he said.

I picked up my ginger ale on the rocks and chinked it with Maysmith's tumbler.

"You did good, sport. Sandstone first. Then Gary," I said, as the embers in Maysmith's eyes grew even redder.

Chapter 14

Sandstone Federal Correctional Institution is a low level security prison located in Sandstone, Minnesota. I had been there once several years ago to interview an inmate on a long-forgotten case but now, gazing at the entrance, it brought back memories of stale-smelling linoleum floors, half-filled mop buckets with stagnant water, sullen-looking guards with sunken brows and a small room with no windows, where the so-called interrogation took place. That was, however, several years ago and I imagined that things had changed, as most things in life do, except one, that decrepitly small interview room with peeling gray paint on the walls and with no windows.

His name was Cani Gashi and he was an ethnic Albanian from Macedonia. His claim to fame was that he was a master of the burning bar, sometimes referred to as a thermic lance, used in cracking safes. He had been a member of an Albanian burglary crew operating out of Staten Island, New York and travelling throughout the country to commit their nefarious deeds but most of the members had been apprehended and convicted for various crimes in New York state and were presently incarcerated in Dannemora State Prison, sequestered among pine trees and loneliness in upstate New York, and a mere stone's throw from the Canadian border.

He was waiting for us when we arrived, compliments of our F.B.I. escort, Agent Brent Rollins, who had the original ticket on a slew of interstate truck hijackings that had landed Gashi in the piss hole where he was presently incarcerated. His latent fingerprints, or as the fingerprint examiner had indicated, partials which were inconclusive, however, had identified Gashi as a possible person of interest in a homicide investigation in Gary, Indiana where an older Macedonian gypsy woman had been murdered. Blue shards of glass had been found at the crime scene and those shards inexplicably had been matched through the F.B.I. glass fragment database to the shards found at the murder scene of Vadoma in Chicago. Coincidence? Not really. In homicide investigations there were no coincidences, just cold hard facts that oftentimes refused to give up their secrets. So that is why Detective Maysmith and myself were in that small room smelling of lost hopes and squandered promises and confronting one misshapen and misguided sociopath, whose facial features could be described as only a black-and-white photograph of abject failure where the ink had run into murky streaks. Agent Rollins was in the leadoff spot on the scorecard and initiated the questioning.

It did not go well. Gashi wanted assurances. In fact, he wanted a complete pass on the homicide investigation in which he was a person of interest. After about an hour of back-and-forth with Agent Rollins I had had about enough of that watermelon-headed miscreant with short stubby arms and a receding hairline that would put Ed Asner to shame.

"Guys, let me have a moment alone with our friend," I said.

"Sure, Sarge," said Maysmith, as Rollins nodded in agreement.

Now there were just two of us in that small room with no windows, one of whom was sitting on a hard wooden bench and handcuffed by his wrist to a metal pole that stretched from floor to ceiling. I walked up to him and removed my handcuffs and flamboyantly wiggled them in front of his face.

"Yeah, right, but I'm already cuffed if ya' haven't noticed," he said with a smirk on his bent-in face.

"Oh, these?" I asked. "They're for something else."

"Like what?"

Holding them tightly by the chain, each manacle protruding from the edges of my hand, I viciously whipped them across his face. While he attempted to stanch the flow of blood with his free hand I grabbed it and cuffed it and then secured the other manacle to the pole.

"Listen, shithead, you have no choice," I said. "Tell me where she's at."

"I ain't tellin' you nothin'."

I grabbed him by the neck with both of my hands. I squeezed as hard as I could, imagining that I was squeezing a head of rotten lettuce. He winced and tried to speak but nothing came out. His face began to turn purple and a gurgling sound followed some white goo that began dripping from his mouth.

"Where is she?" I screamed in his face.

He continued to struggle. I let up a bit so he could speak but nothing came out. I squeezed harder, the veins in my hands pulsating as if they were going to pop. I just kept squeezing. I didn't care if he died. I just didn't care at all about anything but finding her. His eyes bulged a bit at the corners, a sticky phlegm-like mess oozing from his eye sockets. My nails were now sunk deeply into his raw skin. Blood was flowing copiously from the wounds and covering my hands but I just kept squeezing. I felt something hard moving about and recognized it as his hyoid bone. One snap of my wrists and it would be crushed and he would be dead. I let up a bit and then yelled into his face.

"Where is she? Where is Esmeralda, the green-eyed girl?"

He spit something onto the floor. It was thick and black but it wasn't blood. I imagined that it was the stale tar of incarceration. I began to squeeze harder again but I recognized a tell in his eyes that he was going to give it up. I released him from my death grip and sat down in front of him. I riveted my eyes into his as if I was burning a hole in a safe with a burning bar. I read in his eyes that he knew I would kill him.

"Where is she?" I asked one last time.

And he told me.

Chapter 15

If Detective Maysmith was adroit at anything, he was adroit at reading people. I was certain that he read in my eyes that I was mentally exhausted. Maysmith also, however, was pedantically thorough. So I knew on the ride back to Chicago there would be a question or two posed to me.

"So, Sarge, where to next?" he asked.

"Gary, Indiana. She's being held in a house there," I said, not opening my eyes.

"Search warrant?" he asked.

"Right, our friend Rollins will handle it. ITAR something or other," I said.

"I'll alert our guys back in Chicago right away to start drafting it," said Rollins.

I reached into my pocket and handed him some scribbled notes I had made from the so-called interrogation.

"It's all in there. Some crazy shit about an arranged marriage, an abduction, and all the crap that flows along with it," I said.

"ITAR?" asked Maysmith.

"Interstate Travelling in Aid of Racketeering – Kidnapping," said Rollins.

"Got it. Now I know you're spent, Sarge, but just one other question," said Maysmith.

I opened my eyes and looked up at him, my head propped against the window in the backseat.

"That mess back there, you almost killed him. How are we going to explain that?"

"That's an easy one. Myself and two witnesses are going to say that he tried to choke himself to death.

With that, I closed my eyes again. The only thing on my mind was deep green emerald eyes.

Chapter 16

My eyes somewhat opened but things remained blurry. I had cotton-mouth and could barely swallow what moisture remained in my throat. As I blinked my eyes I heard a voice that seemed to be coming from the further reaches of a wind tunnel. It gradually got louder and more coherent and I recognized it as Maysmith's voice.

"Wake up, Sarge," he said. "The worst is over."

"The worst?" I managed to ask, barely able to swallow.

"Here, drink this slowly," said Maysmith, handing me a paper cup filled with water.

"The worst?" I managed to ask again after a few sips.

"Two slugs, 9mm, they got both of them. You were damn lucky they hit the fleshy part of your left leg," said Maysmith.

Then I remembered being number three in the stack making entry, with Maysmith directly behind me and Rollins lead dog on the ram. I remembered hearing the dull thud of the battering ram hitting a soggy wooden door. I remembered the flash-bangs going off and then the sound of sporadic gunfire. I remembered the intense heat sensation in my left leg as I collapsed, falling to the floor. I remembered Maysmith leaning over me, attempting to stanch the wounds, whispering to me to hang on, and then the hot-white excruciating pain hit me and all was dark.

"How long was I out?" I asked.

A nurse in a blue-smock with a nametag that read Lois, and a face that was as severe as the aftermath of the Battle of the Bulge, was adjusting my I.V.

"Two hours in surgery and, well, about an hour in recovery," Lois said, looking at her watch. "How's the pain?"

There was a dull throb in my left leg but the real pain was where the I.V. was attached to the top of my left hand.

"It's my hand," I said.

"We had a little trouble getting the I.V. in," she said, nodding at my left hand. "Seems you have rather thick skin."

"In more ways than one," laughed Maysmith.

Lois took my temperature and then felt my forehead.

"Seems you've stabilized, Detective. No more pain pills for a while," she said and then looking at Maysmith she added, "I suppose it's okay to bring them in."

"Them?" I asked.

The smile across Maysmith's face was as wide as the Mississippi River after a deluge.

"I'll just be a moment," he said, turning to leave as Lois continued to adjust several of the tubes that were connected to the I.V.

She then helped me sit up, propping me up with a pillow behind my back.

"Now only for a few minutes. He needs to rest," Lois said, as Maysmith appeared leading Esmeralda next to where I lay.

In her arms was a small bundle wrapped in a blue blanket, the color of Vadoma's blue window, and that was covered with several long-stemmed red roses.

"They are not blue roses, James, but they do have eight petals," she said.

My eyes that only moments before were as dry as cracked wheat and caked with the crust of a two-hour surgery now flowed copiously with tears of regeneration. Slowly moving the roses away from the top of the bundle, Esmeralda smiled as a small pink face appeared.

"She is yours, James. I call her little Vadoma.

Epilogue

In that peculiar, yet intriguing, realm known as the Wasteland colors can be not only fanciful but important, as well. Take for instance an eight-petalled blue rose. In botanical texts and in natural surroundings you simply won't find this oddity but, dear reader, in the Wasteland all things are possible. If only in one's imagination this floral peculiarity exists, it does, in fact, exist. And so it was here, in a hospital recovery room that lost love was regenerated in the form of one worn-out and thick-skinned police detective and an emerald-eyed beauty born of rambling gypsy caravans winding along steep mountain roads in the dead of night. Then factor into the equation of regeneration and impossibilities one tiny, pink-faced bundle of love known by the name of little Vadoma, well, impossibilities be damned because the name Vadoma means *to know.*

Oh, Vadoma's blue window, you ask? Well, I imagine that once our rough and tough detective is healed, our newly-acquainted and regenerated threesome will find themselves gazing out at a rolling blue-green sea from the comfort of a thatched hut on some exotic out island like Naxos sprinkled among other touristy enclaves in the Aegean Sea. For it is from Naxos, the largest of the Greek Cyclades Islands, where the deep blue color of Vadoma's oval window originated, as the intricate glass pattern was woven with splinters of the Greek blue sapphire which is endemic to that very same island. So from their private abode where there really is no window at all from which to look out, just an open space, there still predominates the intense blue colors resembling lapis and azurite dancing in the distance leading to a never-ending deep blue horizon. So as our hero and heroine, with their little bundle of joy, gaze out of that open space where Vadoma's blue window is only an imagined entity, a mere memory that will never cease to exist, a snippet in time duly passed but certainly not forgotten, and from where only the innate beauty of an indigo horizon is their constant companion that not only soothes their souls but that defies impossibilities, their regeneration will be sealed for all eternity.

Seat 2-B

Chapter 1

"Did you see that?" the driver asked as he cranked his head backwards, almost decapitating himself.

The guard who was riding shotgun likewise swiveled his head in the direction of the frantically waving and half-naked woman.

"Damn! Stop the bus!" screamed the guard.

The look on the driver's face was halfway between lustful curiosity and regretful commitment to his assigned duties, delivering the three unfortunate miscreants, who were shackled to their respective seats, to their newly assigned living quarters in the worst prison in Arizona.

"We're on duty if you haven't forgotten," said the driver, a crusty veteran of prisoner transport who knew every back road and roaming, cattle-encrusted excuse for a highway that canvassed the barrenness and desolation that defined central Arizona.

"For God's sake, take a look at that rack! Stop the damn bus!"

The driver eased up on the gas and then slowly steered the bus to the side of the road about a hundred yards or so in front of the woman who was now in a slow trot and bee-lining for the bus, her large bosoms bouncing in unison like gaudy Christmas baubles with her uneven gait.

The driver unfastened his seatbelt, stood up, and judiciously surveyed his three charges. They were separated by several rows of seats, just to keep things from escalating out of proportion. In the rear of the bus sat Hodgkins, a convicted child molester and consummate pervert. He kept mostly to himself, undoubtedly recreating his sordid past deeds in his mind over and over again and living out each and every deviant fantasy and who, for all intents and purposes, was simply a non-factor in the potential outbreak of mischief. In the middle of the bus sat Wilson, an anarchist who simply hated anyone and everyone. The problem with him was that he was not only devious, he was smart, real smart. The real problem in this panorama of misfits, however, was the convict sitting close to where the guard with the shotgun was seated, Seat 2-B to be exact. His name was Richards and he was a stone-cold, sadistic sociopath, murder-for-hire and mayhem being his so-called calling card.

"I'm going out to take a look-see," said the guard with the shotgun, whose name was Benner, the smile on his face measuring the length of the yard-to-gain marker on first and ten, as he handed the shotgun to the driver whose name was Jimenez.

"Make it short," said Jimenez.

"Right, but keep an eye on Richards. The other two mutts are lost in their kinky daydreams and shouldn't be a problem."

"Check," said the driver, easing down into a sitting position, the business end of the short-barreled Remington 870 shotgun Benner had handed him pointing directly at Richards' midsection but before Benner could exit the bus she was standing at the door and noticeably out of breath.

"My car, my car broke down," she panted, breathing deeply and rapidly. "Over there. It's over there."

Benner looked to where the woman was pointing. An old Ford station wagon with the hood propped up and covered in cattle dust stared back at him but his eyes were soon fixated upon the woman's dancing gewgaws, as she fidgeted nervously and on the verge of tears.

"Ah, ma'am, your blouse, you seem to have misplaced it," said Benner, more than half-leering at her.

"It's the radiator. It overheated and it was so hot, I just took off my blouse and used it to try to get the cap off but ..." she began to sob, as she covered her breasts with her folded arms.

"Alright then, let's go back and take a look-see and maybe we can get you back on the road," said Benner, as he exited the bus and lightly brushed against the woman somewhat on purpose.

Chapter 2

It was a messy crime scene, as crime scenes go; lots of blood and gore, a plethora of bullet holes and blood spatter patterns spaced unevenly across the mosaic of death, some thick, some not so thick. Scattered shell casings, bits of cartilage and bone fragments embedded in seat cushions, and several mangled bodies strewn about completed the death scene and that was just the prison bus.

"Gonna' be several hours," said the crime scene tech, a thickset guy in his late twenties whose I.D. entwined around his neck read Hansen.

"Four dead in all and not one iota of an effort to hide the evidence. It's a disorganized crime scene right out of Investigations 101 and we haven't even got to the other scene down the road," said the detective, pointing toward where the Ford station wagon had been parked but was now only populated by the corpse of Benner.

The detective's name was John Raynor and he had pulled the ticket on the mayhem that cruelly stared up at him, a crime scene scattered over a hundred yards or so of Arizona loneliness.

"Three dead in the bus and one down yonder in the gully," said Hansen, pointing south of where the prison bus had been imbedded in a rather large tuft of sagebrush, half on and half off the road.

"Yeah, that about sums it up," said the detective.

Chapter 3

(1 year later)

"Landslide," said the rancher.

He appeared as old as the bleak canyons littered with rolling sage brush and scattered cacti that surrounded him. His skin was dark and lizard-like, and deeply blistered, compliments of years of prospecting, ranching, and just plain hanging on in this enclave of whistling wind that swept across the barren landscape that surrounded them. His face, that was drawn as taut as thick barbed wire, was as wrinkled as a grooms' tuxedo after the reception had ended. His voice was deep and seeded with the plethora of years that he had survived in this godforsaken wilderness of sporadic rattlesnakes, crawling centipedes and the occasional coyote lingering among the carcasses of dead cattle but his eyes were the mirror to his soul. They appeared deadpan and lifeless, and as dark as his blistered skin, but he spoke with a certain calculated urgency, characteristic of the low arousal psychopaths have claimed as their dominion over the centuries. So as he stood steadfast and with arms folded, he waited for Raynor's reply.

"How so?" asked Detective Raynor.

"Indian kids from the reservation over yonder. Playing with some old dynamite they found from a boarded-up mine.

Damn near blew up half of the damn mountain," said the rancher, his lips covered with streaks of brown scum, the color of the dirt road on which he stood.

He crudely spit a glob of Redman Chewing Tobacco onto the road, wiped his mouth with the sleeve of his tattered flannel shirt that was coated with fresh tobacco stains and that smelled of cattle dung. Then he pointed over his shoulder to a pile of large boulders that appeared strategically placed in front of an opening to a small cave.

"Over there. Damn funny how them boulders fell down and landed kinda' in a nice little line but you'll find it inside. Didn't touch a damn thing, just left it where it was. Never know if them things are bobby-trapped. Learned that lesson in Nam. If you don't know, don't go, 'cause it might blow," he said, tipping the bill of his wind-worn cap, which was about as old as he was and which read U.S Army Rangers.

Raynor motioned to the two evidence techs standing behind him to follow him and when they got to the entrance of the cave Raynor stopped and then looked inside. In the faint light from the ever-present sun peeking through the mackerel-colored sky of an autumn Arizona morning he strained to see the outline of a vehicle. His heart skipped a beat. Could it be the same vehicle for which he'd been searching for the past year?

"Light it up, boys," he said, turning to the two criminalists who waited at his side, their flashlights at the ready, their digging tools lying on the ground next to where they stood.

"Seen your flyer posted in the country store over at the crossroads. About a year or so ago, it was. Kept it just in case. Arizona State Police, that's you," said the rancher.

Raynor remembered being in the area about a year ago, a week or two after the mayhem on the prison bus had occurred, and personally passing out flyers that requested any information on strange vehicles seen in the area. The crime scene search had turned up tire tracks in the dusty road about a hundred yards or so from where the prison bus had been driven into a ditch on the side of the road. It had appeared that the unknown vehicle had departed the area at a high rate of speed, as evidenced by the deep-set and discolored tire tracks left on the road, as well as over the mangled body of one of the correctional officers, a twenty-year veteran named Ralph Benner. The Arizona State Crime Lab had identified the tire tracks as coming from the type of tires associated with Ford station wagons from years gone by but that's with all that they could come up. Now Raynor was peering into the darkness of a forbidden cave, hoping against hope that the vehicle entrapped inside of it was the vehicle for which he'd been searching for the past year or so, and that finally some answers would be forthcoming.

"Watch out for trip wires, boys," said Raynor, as the two evidence techs flashing their light beams into the dark cave moved forward.

Within seconds they were back out.

"Gonna' need more light, something stationary, so we can get a better look. It's a station wagon. No doubt about that but the front end is still covered with rocks. Gonna' have to dig it out," said the evidence tech whose name was Johnson.

"How long?" asked Raynor.

"About as long as it will take to get a rig up here and pull the damn thing out," said the second evidence tech, whose name was also Johnson but no relation to the first criminalist.

"How about my tractor? It's got a damn big winch on it," said the rancher, smiling as if a payday was in the offing.

Interpreting the rancher's grin, Raynor nodded.

"Good idea. We'll reimburse you for your expenses. How long?" asked Raynor.

"Not too long," said the rancher, spitting a glob of discolored chew onto the road, almost hitting a crawling red centipede. "Hate them damn things."

Chapter 4

"I see you got lucky," said Raynor's boss, Captain Juan Santiago.

"In some respects, yes. It's the car, all right. Found a Remington 870 shotgun stuffed in the trunk under some old blankets and an old .38 caliber revolver next to it. Now we just have to wait for ballistics to match up the evidence. Dusted everything we could for latents but buried in a cave for over a year, well, roll the dice on that score."

"DNA?" asked Santiago.

"That too. Swabbed everything real good. Got some possibilities but it's a waiting game now. You know how backlogged the lab is," said Raynor.

"Anything else?"

"Pulled the tires. Preliminary information from the lab indicates a match to the marks in the road and the impressions left on Benner's chest. We have DMV chasing down the registration of the vehicle but it appears they tried to scratch off the VIN. If I were a betting guy, which I'm not, I'd wager that those boys down at the lab will bring something up. Probably stolen anyway. It's a piece of garbage and it could have been purchased at a junk yard or at an auto wrecker's. We're checking out those angles, as we speak."

"Purchased for cash, no doubt. I doubt if you'll find a record," said Santiago.

"Right," said Raynor.

"Keep your fingers crossed on the DNA swabs. I'll bet my pension it's our guy, Richards."

"But somebody helped him, somebody driving that piece of shit that was probably used as a ruse to get the prison bus to stop. You know as well as I do that those guys have strict orders not to stop."

"So what would make them stop?" asked Santiago, fiddling with some papers on his desk.

They both looked each other square in the eyes.

"Not Jiminy Cricket," said Raynor.

"Right, more like Snow White," said Santiago, a half-assed police grin forming at the corners of his mouth.

"Right, presently we're checking out girlfriends, wives, ex-wives and paramours of Richards," said Raynor. "Could get lucky there."

"You did that already, didn't you?" asked Santiago.

"Several times over, yes, but all negative. It appears that the guy is a loner, probably satisfying his sexual needs with one-night stands from strip joint to strip joint. Follow me?"

"Check," said Santiago.

"Anything else, boss?" asked Raynor.

"Yeah, roll the dice," said Santiago.

Chapter 5

She looked in the mirror. She didn't see what she wanted to see. She then looked at her cell phone. No answers were forthcoming from either. She took in a deep breath and adjusted her sagging breasts as she prepared to go on stage. It would be the last dance of the night and maybe some good tips would be stuffed into her garters and bra. She looked back in the mirror but no answers were forthcoming. She hated herself. She looked back at the cell phone. Damn it, he ran out on her again and now she needed money. She'd make the call as soon as she was done with her so-called performance, baring her breasts for a handful of broken-down ranch hands and drifters, and other assorted losers and misfits, that lived out their fantasies by carnally possessing her in their minds. She looked back at her cell phone and then forlornly at her purse, which was as empty as her virginity was dissipated. It contained no money, only the flyer the police had left at the strip joint where she eked out an existence. Damn him. He shouldn't have left her so alone.

Chapter 6

Arizona State Prison Complex (Florence, Arizona) – 10 years later

It was a small room and quite crowded. The Director of the Department of Corrections stood stoically with his arms folded as the would-be onlookers began seating themselves. Richards had no friends and no known family members, so that factor in the equation of whom would be present was eliminated. It was simply a zero-sum game for Richards when it came to people on whom he could count, so the remaining seats were simply being filled by twelve reputable citizens of Arizona, compliments of the Director's selection.

Detective Raynor was there, of course, being the detective assigned to the case, and he was presently engaged in a conversation with a priest detailed to the prison from a nearby Catholic church, the prison chaplain, his mentor, occupying a seat in the execution chamber proper. Raynor turned to the priest and read utter dejection in his clouded eyes.

"Awful, simply awful," said the young priest, shaking his head and wringing his hands.

"Well, Father, it's been going on in Arizona since 1910, one-hundred executions thus far," said Raynor bluntly.

The dejected priest only shook his head again as he looked through the one-way window into the execution chamber. Richards was being strapped down onto a gurney, the medical attendants at his side preparing the deadly concoction of drugs that would send him to his maker and final resolution on the plain of good and evil.

"Well, at least it's painless," offered Raynor.

But before the humble priest could respond there was a slight bit of commotion at the entranceway to the viewing room. Raynor recognized her immediately, although it had been several years since their last encounter. He really hadn't expected her to come when he had personally sent her an invitation provided by the Director. Now, however, their eyes met on the plain of good and evil in that desolate enclave they both knew and understood as the Wasteland.

"Right this way, Miss," said the crisply attired prison guard, his pants neatly pressed, his white shirt immaculate.

The guard was stoically standing at the door as she handed him a small admittance card, compliments of the Director.

As she carefully moved through the muddle of witnesses to the only unoccupied seat in the small room, she looked up at Raynor with shallow and hollow eyes. It was as if she had not expected to see him there.

"Right, here, ma'am," said the guard, indicating the empty seat.

The lights in the room dimmed slightly as the Director announced that they were about to begin and as she uncomfortably shifted in her seat, Seat 2-B of the viewing room.

Epilogue

One could strongly argue that in the bizarre realm known as the Wasteland there is a Seat 2-B waiting for everyone. It is really a simple choice when one encounters such a situation, strive for social responsibility and just move on with one's life or choose the path to self-perdition and plop one's derriere onto the seat of truth or consequences, and then pray that the inevitable simply won't happen.

And so it was here, in that enigmatic domain known as the Wasteland, that Brent Lee Richards, Inmate #21445, Arizona State Prison, his calling card mayhem and murder for hire, found himself involuntarily seated in a makeshift Seat 2-B of his own making, which was disguised as a stiff metal gurney where a trilogy of lethal injections would soon be administered. Albeit the result of a plethora of unfortunate choices made over a lifetime of criminal behavior he, nonetheless, had orchestrated his own fate.

As far as Miss Loraine, part-time girlfriend and full-time stripper, and most recently dubbed police informant and beneficiary of immunity, well, her seat is less problematic, at least when final outcomes are concerned. It appears that she simply has done the right thing, albeit being an accomplice to murder before and after the fact. Conspiracy theories oftentimes can be complicated but when dropping a dime enters into the equation, and the spilling of beans is factored into the mix of the confused matrix of criminal justice, past transgressions can be, shall we say, swept under the rug of immunity from prosecution.

So, dear reader, as you progress along the undulating tightrope of life's choices, Seat 2-B awaits you. It is your choice, and yours alone, whether you will partake of its misery or simply move on to bigger and better things because simply waiting for the next conundrum in the mysterious realm known as the Wasteland to confront you will certainly lead to bad outcomes.

Book 1

The Wooden Doors
of Santa Sabina

Chapter 1

"Abandon all hope, ye who enter here!"
The Divine Comedy – Dante

"She sees visions, Father," the altar boy mumbled.

"What?" the priest asked.

"Visions," said the boy, his voice somewhat muffled by his smallish hands, pale white and shaking, his face upturned as if he had just seen a ghost.

"Visions? What kind of visions?"

The boy's eyes were tightly closed, spiderwebs forming at the edges. He appeared comatose, as if in a trance at a seance. The priest touched him. The boy was cold and stiff. It was as if *rigor mortis* had set in within a matter of seconds. The priest frantically felt for a pulse – none. He placed his fingers under the boy's nose – cold, dormant. He worriedly reached for a vial of holy water, for his rosary, for anything holy but an uncalming feeling suddenly came over him. It was as if the sacristy was filled with an unexplained dread. The gates to Hell had closed and a stagnant void of suffering seeped in, as the boy's muffled and trembling voice reverberated in the back of the priest's head – *"Visions, Father. She sees visions."*

Chapter 2

"Quite unfortunate," said the Monsignor. "Quite unfortunate, indeed."

Unfortunate, yes, but what of the look that was on the boy's face when he stopped breathing, when he closed his eyes and when he …

"Father, do you agree? Just an unfortunate situation, hmm? Nothing more than that."

"I should have had some holy water with me," the priest said. "At least I could have …"

The Monsignor interrupted him with his ancient finger softly touching his own lips as if he were about to turn a page in a hymnal.

"Holy water is only water, Father William, unless it is in the hands of someone holy," said the Monsignor in somewhat of a pedantic manner. "It is only a mere prop in the hands of a non-believer."

The priest considered the admonition as somewhat of a personal affront.

"Are you insinuating, Monsignor, that I am …"

The Monsignor's gnarled and brown-spotted hand was now in the air, air that permeated with anything but perceived holiness between the two men-of-the-cloth. It stopped the priest from speaking in mid-sentence.

"You are a priest, Father William, and a priest by any definition one would choose is ingrained with holiness. Holiness is deep-seated within you unless, of course, you have strayed from the Church. You are a priest to your God and Father but if you have chosen another path, well, then adjustments must be made."

The priest was caught off-guard by the Monsignor's unabashed accusations but were they, in fact, accusations? Possibly they were only simple observations. The priest had been having second thoughts about his vocation, having only been ordained for a few short months. Perhaps it was evident to one so skilled in observing human behavior and, more importantly, human failings. The priest's self-effacement, with respect to his priestly duties, had seemed to be fading away. Before he could dwell further on his own shortcomings, the Monsignor had pushed an envelope across his desk to the priest who was sitting upright in a straight-backed and uncomfortable chair.

"Open it, please, Father," said the Monsignor.

Father William feared that he was being released from his priestly position. With somewhat trembling hands, he slowly opened the curious missive. It was a roundtrip ticket to Rome.

"Rome?" he asked, considerably perplexed.

"Yes, I have arranged for a short sabbatical for you. You will depart tomorrow. Father Morrison will meet you when you arrive."

"And then what?" the priest asked.

"You will assist Father Morrison with cataloging the numerous letters that the Church has received over the years but that have never been reviewed, some of which have never been opened. You will be there about a month."

"And where is there, Monsignor?"

"The Basilica of Saint Sabina. It is a historical church located on the Aventine Hill near Rome. It is the mother church of the Roman Catholic Order of Preachers, the Dominicans, and if you haven't forgotten, Father William, we are preachers at heart and that is our order."

The priest felt trapped in a wilderness of doubt, doubt as to his priestly calling, doubt as to whom he really was and, most importantly, doubt as to what the outcome in all of this would be.

"And one other thing, Father William, please, closely examine the panels of the doors of Saint Sabina. Perhaps in them you will regain your concept of holiness."

The Monsignor's eyes were a dull gray, narrowly opened, and penetrating, as if he had had his fill of sin and filth throughout his fifty odd years as a man-of the cloth.

"Yes, Monsignor, but what of the young boy of whom we spoke earlier and the unknown girl with the visions?" the priest asked.

"Perhaps when you have regained your holiness, if in fact you have lost it, perhaps then we will revisit that anomaly."

Chapter 3

"Saint Sabina is honored on the 29th day of August and again with Saint Serapia on the third day of September. It is on that day that a famous ancient church was dedicated to God in Rome in 430 A.D. under the patronage of those two saints"
Basilica of Saint Sabina in Rome

The Aventine Hill in Rome is one of several hills on which the ancient city was built. The Basilica of Saint Sabina in Rome is situated on this hill with a spectacular view of the surrounding holy places that are endemic to this distinctively pristine enclave of spirituality. Father William sat on a wide brick wall the color of dried clay. It was a wall that overlooked the many buildings and structures, and the deep green foliage of the surrounding trees and shrubbery, that defined this place, this place where he hoped to regain the holiness that somehow had slowly seeped from his soul. Father Morrison stood next to him, arms folded, as if the spectacular beauty was to be taken for granted and as if he had viewed it *ad nauseum* and now was simply imbued with the intention of getting on with the work to be done with his new protégé.

"Spectacular," said Father William.

"You will get used to it," said Father Morrison with a distinctly Irish brogue to his accent.

"Used to it? I doubt that, Father. The holiness of this area is overpowering. No, I will never get used to it, as you say, Father," said Father William.

Father Morrison was quite older than Father William, who was only several months out of the seminary and approaching his 24th birthday. Father Morrison had reached that epic feat at least twice. He was slouched-shouldered and had a receding hairline, dull brown strands of hair needing a good clipping hanging over his misshapen ears. His eyes were dark, sunken and hidden somewhat by shadows. He appeared to Father William as an unhappy and perplexed man. Perhaps, like Father William, he was struggling to regain his holiness that somehow had abandoned him along his life's journey or, perhaps, he had just given up hope.

"You are here for a reason, Father William. Your concept of holiness is involved, I believe. It is now time that we address that reason and get to work, hmm," said Father Morrison, turning to leave and indicating that it was time to abandon the view of holiness and begin the view of opening letter upon letter to the Church of which the good Monsignor had so eloquently spoken.

Father William arose and then looked to his right. Two young lovers were sitting on the same wall where he had been seated. They were clutching each other in an embrace that Father William could only imagine as equating to true love. The sky above them was filled with gray-white clouds, obscuring the sun. It was a warm day and the lovers were sleeveless. Then a sudden uneasiness began to manifest itself in the priest's entrails. He envied them but wasn't envy a sin? Envy: *"A feeling of discontented or resentful longing aroused by someone else's possessions, qualities, or luck."* Yes, he realized that he did, in fact, envy them. He then began thinking about falling in love, as his concept of holiness seeped further from his soul, but priests were not supposed to fall in love, were they?

"Are you coming, Father?" asked Father Morrison.

Chapter 4

*"Bring me out of prison, that I may
give thanks to thy name!*
The Holy Bible, Psalms 142:7

It was a moonless night, his first night in Rome in his journey to regain his holiness. The priest's mind was not focused on holiness, however, it was focused on the two lovers immersed in each other's arms that he had observed earlier in the day. What were they doing now, he wondered? Envy somehow began to creep back into the picture. He quickly dismissed that thought from the back of his mind. Suddenly he felt like a stranger in a strange country. Father Morrison had retired early to bed, yet Father William remained restless, sitting on a bark caftan chair on the small portico to his room and looking up at the unforgiving dark and moonless sky. He wanted out of this damn prison of encumbered holiness. He wanted the chains to be broken and his emotions to be set free and unfettered with unwarranted guilt. He roughly grabbed his jacket, as the night air had cooled, and he decided to rid himself of dwelling on thoughts of despair. He just began walking to nowhere in particular.

Soon he was walking along a back alley a mile or so from where the rectory was located behind the church. It was a narrow alley but rather well-lit for the time of evening. It was in a bazaar-like atmosphere that he found himself wandering with shop after shop lining the alleyway and selling trinkets and religious paraphernalia distinctive of the region. Couples were meandering about hand-in-hand, stealing a kiss here and there, and giggling as lovers do and soon his mind was dwelling on how happy they probably were, as well as on the other side of the ill-fated coin, how miserably lonely he actually was.

He did not want to end up like Father Morrison, unkept, stoop-shouldered, and with straggly mousy brown hair flapping over his ears. Perhaps that is what happens to a person who has never experienced true love but, on the other hand, could holiness bridge that gap? Perhaps if he rediscovered his lost holiness, if he could somehow suck it back into his soul, then maybe he would not wind up like that old and broken-down priest. He stopped at one of the curio shops and began to peruse some postcards that were for sale. He picked one up and regarded it at eye-level. It depicted the ornate doors of Saint Sabina and then the words of the good Monsignor were resurrected from his memories. *"Please, closely examine the panels of the doors of Saint Sabina. Perhaps in them you will regain your concept of holiness."*

"Would you like that one, Father," she asked in English with a distinctive Italian flavor to her speech.

Father? Then he remembered he had not removed his white collar and, as his jacket was slightly unzipped, he realized it was somewhat exposed.

"Yes, yes, I will take it," the priest said.

"It is a holy place, Father," she said. "I have heard that lost souls go there to regain their holiness. They simply place their hands on the panels of the sacred doors. I have been there often. Have you been there?"

She was at least twice his age and somewhat overweight. Her eyes were dark brown like old walnuts and appeared sad. She was dressed in a rather non-descript, long black dress that reached to her ankles where a pair of old and worn sandals completed the ensemble of what the priest envisioned as simply impoverished endurance.

"Not yet, Signora, but I will soon," the priest said as he removed his wallet from his pocket.

She then clapped her hands loudly and a young woman slowly emerged from the back of the kiosk through a waterfall of colored beads that hung from floor to ceiling in the doorway.

"No need for that, Father," said the older woman. "Leonora will wrap it for you."

She then turned to the younger woman and whispered something in her ear, and then was lost from the priest's sight disappearing into whatever mysteries were concealed behind the waterfall of colored beads.

"I'll wrap that for you, Father," Leonora said in perfect English, reaching for the postcard.

The priest was tongue-tied and it was not from her perfect English. It was from the perfection in her smile, in the flawlessness in her twinkling violet eyes, in the perfect curvature of her hips, in the symmetry of her ruby-red lips, in the lyrical sound of her soft voice in …

"Father, I'll wrap it for you but you must give it to me first," she laughed slightly.

The priest then realized that he was tightly holding her hand over the picture postcard. He sheepishly let go of his grip.

"Sorry, I was just …"

"The doors of Saint Sabina can do that to a person," she said. "I'll just be a moment."

She disappeared behind the waterfall of colored beads but the priest was not thinking of colored beads, nor of waterfalls. He was thinking of the lovely Leonora and so it began.

Chapter 5

"For when dreams increase, empty words
grow many; but do you fear God?"
The Holy Bible, Ecclesiastes 5:7

"Your collar, Father, have you misplaced it?" Leonora asked, a sultry, yet circumspect, grin on her angelic face.

Misplaced? Intentionally not worn would be more *apropos*.

"You are quite perceptive, Leonora. I seemed to have forgotten it today," the priest lied.

She smiled at him, the twinkle in her violet eyes walking the tight rope of truth or consequences.

"You are not here to purchase more picture postcards are you, Father?" she subtly asked.

The priest's legs were quaking, as if he had just been hit with a round of buckshot from a short-barreled Remington 870 shotgun. He righted the ship of his misgivings, unfurled the ensign, drew anchor and made way. Damn it all, she was more perceptive than he imagined her to be.

"No, Leonora, I am here to see you," he said flatly.

"But you are a priest, Father, and I am but a 22-year old student of philosophy at a more or less average college in the area."

"Yes, that is true but …"

She waved her hand in the air, cautioning him to stop speaking.

"Your collar is like a wedding ring, Father. Married men on the prowl typically remove it from their fingers before engaging potential lovers in discourse. Is that what is happening here? Are you on the prowl, Father? Am I a potential lover or are your words to me empty words?"

"Damn it, stop calling me Father. My name is William," the priest said. "And my words are from my heart."

"But you do fear God, don't you? You are a priest after all," she said.

He'd convinced himself that he really didn't want to be a priest anymore. He simply wanted to be in love. Why did it fall on him anyway? Sure he was the eighth child in a family of nine in a traditional Catholic family where someone had to enter into religious seclusion. None of his sisters chose to do so, which left him and his three remaining brothers to toe the line. Marty, however, was soon eliminated, felony convictions for extortion can do that to a guy. Johnny, his parents' favorite, earned his MBA and was simply more concerned with making a buck than with saving souls. That left just himself and his older brother, Pete, who simply got a girl pregnant in high school and, well, that was the end of that. It seemed that he had drawn the short straw and now he was in Rome, lonely as hell, and falling in love with a young woman who knew absolutely nothing about him. Holiness be damned. He was going to do what his mind and soul dictated and if it cast his soul into the confines of the bottomless pit, so be it.

"I am only human," the priest said.

"I knew as much," she said, taking the priest's hand and gently holding it to her face. "I knew as much."

Her lips were on his. His senses were somewhere on a pendulum swinging in midair in no specific direction. Fortune was turning her wheel, its destination unknown, and he was lost in an illusion of what the definition of love should be.

But all was short-lived, as he found himself sitting starkly upright in his bed, the lazy rays from the morning sun dancing through the window and casting their light upon his face. Having awakened him and leaving a sunken feeling in the pit of his stomach, the rays from the sun slowly receded, as the priest felt the holiness in his soul following suit.

Chapter 6

"Then I saw an angel coming down from heaven, holding in his hand the key of the bottomless pit and a great chain."
The Holy Bible, Revelations 20:1

She was standing by the small kiosk when he approached it. It was early evening, the gloaming from the incipient clouds of night carpeting a velvet sky. With the long day of letter reading in the basement of the rectory behind him, he felt extraordinarily refreshed when he saw her. She appeared to see him instantly, a smile birthing on her face where only moments before only a blank expression was apparent to the priest.

"Good evening, Father William," she said. "Coming back for more picture postcards of the wooden doors of Santa Sabina?" she modestly asked.

She was wearing a long black dress with a darker belt having a silver buckle. Her dress reached to the tops of her ankles and did not cover her sandals, the color of the sky above, which was a deep velvet. In each of her ears were gold hoop earrings the size of quarters that moved precociously as she laughed. Her eyes were a deep violet, mimicking the sky above them and almost black, and danced with the gaiety of a young woman who was about to discover the mysterious concept of love. Her upturned lips, devoid of lip gloss, were invented for kissing, thought the priest but whether that endeavor would ever take place with him as a participant was mere conjecture bordering on the impossible.

"Father, are you daydreaming?"

The priest was caught off-guard and somewhat embarrassed.

"Just thinking, Leonora. I've been reading letters addressed to the Church all day. Some of them must have stuck in the back of my head," he said.

"You must think of the Church a lot," she said, handing him a picture postcard. "I think that you will like this one."

The priest took the postcard from dainty hands and perused it as if it were the Holy Grail. The scent from her perfume was somewhat emanating from it. The fragrance of sweet lilacs held him in rapture as he looked at the postcard.

"Have you had the chance to look through the keyhole?" she asked.

The postcard depicted the Aventine Keyhole.

"It is quite beautiful," said the priest. "But, no, I have not yet had the chance," he said.

"Oh, but you must," she said, her eyes dancing with enthusiasm. "The keyhole is found on an ordinary green door. The view is from a decorative brass keyhole found on that same door," she said.

"And what will one observe?" asked the priest.

"What you will see is the land beyond and that land comprises the countries of Italy, Malta and the sovereign of Vatican City. You see, Father William, three countries are visible from just that small keyhole. You will also see a flawlessly miniature view of Saint Peter's Basilica, which is divinely framed by vibrant, green leafy hedges that line a narrow pathway in the priory, which is known as the Piazza of the Knights of Malta."

"And where is it located, this keyhole?" asked the priest, while he looked into her eyes, hoping that she would escort him there.

"The door with the keyhole is found on an unpretentious piazza, *Piazza dei Calvieri di Malta*, the Piazza of the Knights of Malta of which I just spoke. It is located on a hillside above the River Tiber and on the southernmost of the seven hills surrounding Rome."

"I see," said the priest.

"I can take you there, Father, and we can look through the keyhole together. It is an old Roman legend that if two souls look out from the keyhole together, well, their hearts become one."

The priest's heart was pumping uncontrollably as he felt her dark violet eyes upon his.

"Or if you prefer, Father, we can view the *Giardina de Aravci*, the Orange Garden of Rome. It is quite spectacular, as well," she said, handing the priest another postcard depicting the self-same garden.

But the priest wasn't listening. He was dwelling upon looking out of that mysterious keyhole with Leonora, their cheeks touching, and the heat from their respective bodies kindling a dormant fire in his soul that the priest believed was about to ignite into an inferno of forbidden love.

"Father, which one have you chosen?" she asked, a certain impatience in her eyes, a certain longing that the priest was unable to quantify.

"The keyhole, of course," said the priest.

"Excellent choice. Tomorrow is Saturday and I am free all day. I will be ready at 8:00 a.m. We must leave early, Father, to avoid the crowds. I will be waiting for you here," she said.

With that she disappeared behind the rainbow of colored beads, leaving Father William holding the postcard depicting the Aventine Keyhole. He clutched it desperately to his heart, as if to lose it would somehow seal his ill-conceived fate.

As he walked back to the rectory he suddenly felt an uneasiness in the depths of his stomach. It were as if an angel of the Lord had descended upon him holding a key, a key to the bottomless pit, along with a great chain, and not the key to the Aventine Keyhole. The key that the angel held, he dejectedly realized, would not fit the Aventine Keyhole but, rather, it would fit the keyhole to his demise if he crossed the line of perceived holiness and, cheek to cheek, gazed through the keyhole which was reserved for fervent lovers.

Chapter 7

"You shall not commit adultery"
The Holy Bible, Exodus 20:14

Adultery: Extramarital sex that is considered objectionable on social, religious or moral grounds.

The priest struggled with the definition of the word *extramarital*. It stuck in his craw like unrelenting twisting vines. It gnawed at him like so many pesky gnats on a hot humid August night. It assaulted his midbrain like an incipient headache that would not go away. He tried to convince himself that the word just didn't fit him, nor did it fit what he anticipated happening. He wasn't married and neither was Leonora. So extramarital sex was not about to occur, if sex occurred at all. After all, it would be consensual sex anyway but was he, in so many unspoken words, married to the Church? Would that then qualify him as an adulterer and subject him to excommunication and to expulsion into the bottomless pit, as an angel of the Lord with a hideous and unholy grin plastered across its angelic face, while swinging a long chain and holding a key to lock him away forever, castigated him as an adulterer who had defiled the Lord his Savior?

"I'm ready," she said, emerging from behind the rainbow-colored beads.

She was wearing a pair of tight-fitting Italian blue jeans, a type of skinny push-up pants that stopped just above her ankles, and a loose-fitting white short-sleeved blouse. It was quite warm, a typical sun-drenched August day in Rome. Her long dark hair was neatly wrapped in a tight bun underneath her colorful sun hat.

"You look lovely today," said Father William.

She flashed the priest a coquettish grin.

"You seem to have forgotten your white collar, Father," she said playfully, reaching for his hand.

"It is quite warm today, Leonora, and I've opted instead for an open shirt," the priest said, gently taking her hand.

"It is a short bus ride to our destination and then, dear Father William, we will look together through the Aventine Keyhole," she said, as they walked hand-in-hand to the nearby bus stop.

Once on the bus and seated comfortably next to each other, she turned toward the priest with a mischievous look in her lovely violet eyes.

"Why are you here, Father? Why have you come to Rome?" she asked, her hand gently squeezing his to signal that white lies were not to be tolerated.

"I have come to help at the Church, as I told you. The many letters from the faithful must be answered and I have been chosen to assist in that endeavor," said Father William.

"But all the way from America just to open letters?" she asked

Damn it all. He didn't want to feel like a priest today. Leaving his white collar back at the priory was a beginning but now this. He felt the holiness from his soul having left him, the holiness that he came to Rome in the first place to recover, a concept of holiness she could not understand because she simply was not fitted with that yoke, that yoke of unmerciful dread if he, in fact, did not recover his holiness.

"Today, Leonora, just call me William," said the priest, a light smile on his face.

She squeezed his hand a little tighter and then she laid her head on his chest, which was somewhat heaving in anticipation of being cheek to cheek with her and looking through the Aventine Keyhole.

Chapter 8

"Greet one another with a holy kiss,"
The Holy Bible, 2 Corinthians 13:12

He had never kissed a woman until today. Sure, he had kissed his grandmother and his mother, and his sisters and a plethora of aunts and great aunts, but never a woman in the sense of a man and a woman, in the sense of Adam and Eve and the Tree of Good and Evil in the Garden, or was it the Tree of Truth and Consequences? Maybe there were consequences involved but he just wasn't thinking straight. That kiss, that singular, solitary first kiss was changing his life but would it become only a fond memory he would never forget, a memory that would be ingrained in his very soul for all of eternity? He convinced himself that memory would last forever. It would not dissolve in the dusts of eternity. It would not be erased from his soul but would it only be a simple memory lasting in perpetuity? A simple memory, but that kiss, could it be something more than a mere memory? Could it be the harbinger of the birthing of unbridled love? He caught himself in mid-thought. He had procrastinated long enough.

He held the small missive in his hand that Leonora had given to him as the day trip had ended and when they had returned to her small kiosk. After giving the priest a tender kiss on his cheek, the second of the afternoon, he detected a rather sad smile manifest itself across her otherwise cheerful face

"Good evening, William. It was such a lovely day," she had said, disappearing behind the waterfall of colorful beads.

Now that tiny missive was burning a hole in his hand and soon he feared that it would be burning a hole in his heart. He dreaded that if he opened it his soul would disintegrate into ashes. It were as if he knew what the message contained. He was on his portico and seated in a straight backed chair as before and looking again into a desolate and moonless night, a forbidding night, a solemn omen of what he feared was soon to transpire. He opened the letter and began to read. The letter was written in perfect cursive.

> *"Dear, Father William: I will cherish the fond memories of our time together. It is late August and I must return to my collegiate studies. I will never forget you. Please, keep me in your memories and in your prayers.* Signed – *Leonora.*

It was like a stake driven through his heart. The priest's resolve sunk to the lowest depths of his soul. Discovered love, but for such a short time, was relegated to a mere memory, a snippet of reality that he would simply have to tuck away in his back pocket for those moments when abject loneliness overcame him. Tears did not flow from his eyes. No, his eyes were hardened like deadened steel. He would not succumb to those pent-up emotions begging for release. He would, instead, do what the good Monsignor had bid him to do and, possibly, he would regain the true concept of whom he really was. *"Please, closely examine the panels of the doors of Saint Sabina. Perhaps in them you will regain your concept of holiness."*

Chapter 9

"So also, when you see all these things, you
know that he is near, at the very gates,"
The Holy Bible, Matthew 24:33

It was early morning and the emerging sun was just beginning to cast its lazy rays upon the panels of the wooden doors of Santa Sabina that stared back at him as if he was a non-believer. *"Please, closely examine the panels of the doors of Saint Sabina. Perhaps in them you will regain your concept of holiness."* The Monsignor's words were breathing fire into his soul. He laid his hands upon the panel depicting the crucifixion. He then ran his hands over the intricately carved figure of the Savior, shadowed on each side by the good thief and the bad thief, respectively. He tried to imagine the pain. He tried to devolve the energy from the holiness he perceived as emanating from the abject suffering involved. He wanted that energy, that holiness, to enter his soul. Lost love be damned. That was a feeling of selfishness. Envy be damned, as well. He cast them to the bottomless pit of his misgivings.

He didn't know how long he had been there. He was on his knees and he was crying when Father Morrison found him. His eyes were beet red and swollen, as if he had been weeping for hours. Father Morrison lifted him up by his shoulders. He looked deeply into the priest's bloated eyes.

"It is a good thing you have done, Father William. I believe you have knocked on the gates and have been admitted as a fervent believer who has rediscovered the true concept of holiness. Now let us proceed to the rectory. There are more letters to read."

Chapter 10

"The Spirit of the Lord is upon me to preach good news to the poor. He has sent me to proclaim release to the captives and recovering of sight to the blind, to set at liberty those who are oppressed."
The Holy Bible, Luke 4:18

"It's been about a month that you have been away, Father William," said the Monsignor.

"Yes, I arrived late last night," said Father William.

The Monsignor was seated behind his desk. He appeared even smaller than the last time the priest had seen him, yet his sad eyes remained as listless and soupy gray as before.

"Were you successful, Father?" he delicately asked.

Getting right to the damn point, is he? Well, he fell in love, didn't he? That, in and of itself, was successful. There is nothing immoral about falling in love, is there? But that uncertain holiness thing, well, that was an altogether different matter. He didn't feel unholy. Father Morrison had convinced him of that. That was for sure but had he done something immoral? Possibly, if one were to slice and dice it and Monday morning quarterback the living ins-and-outs of it but hell with all of that and the good Monsignor's sense of immorality. After all, deep down in his very soul, he truly believed he was a moral person. He was certain of that and by running his hands over the ornate panels of the doors to Saint Sabina he truly believed that he, in essence, had rediscovered his lost holiness.

"Yes, Monsignor, I believe I have revived my holiness," he said.

"Well, then let us proceed and continue with God's work, shall we?" he said.

"Yes," said Father William. "Now I believe it is time to revisit the situation with the unknown girl who apparently saw visions, the girl about whom we spoke the last time I was with you."

"Ah, yes, Father, but she is not unknown anymore," said the good Monsignor.

"How so?" the priest asked.

"She is living with nuns," he said.

"Well, that is a good start," said the priest. "At least she is in a holy place."

"She is living in Gaza City in the occupied territories. She is assisting the nuns there and she hopes to become one someday. She is only 16-years old."

"Gaza City?" asked Father William, completely caught unawares.

"She is at the Holy Family Church of Gaza. It is the only Catholic church in Gaza City. It is run by the Congregation of the Incarnate Word. There are two primary schools and two secondary schools there and about two-hundred needy souls who are parishioners. Father Stephen is the Vicar. They also operate a small clinic and it is there where you will find her. Her name is Serapia."

"And she is studying to become a nun?" asked Father William.

"Yes, there are three orders of nuns that are affiliated with the church there, the Sisters of the Incarnate Word, the Sisters of Charity of Mother Teresa and, lastly, the Rosary Sisters. They minister to the sick, disabled and elderly of the region regardless of religious affiliation. It is an arduous task, Father."

"And she is the one who sees visions?" asked Father William.

"Yes."

The Monsignor then slowly slid an envelope across his desk to the priest.

"Please, open it, Father," he said.

The priest did so, not exactly knowing what was entailed in such a gesture. It contained a one-way ticket to Gaza City.

"You will leave tomorrow evening, Father. The Archbishop has approved your travel and, having regained your holiness as you have said, I have full confidence that you can alleviate the situation with the young woman."

Father William looked up and saw only dark gray and listless eyes and possibly a twinkle or two of forlorn hope in the ancient cleric's stare.

"One other thing, Father," said the Monsignor.

"Yes."

"The young woman is blind."

Book 2
Eyeless in Gaza

Chapter 1

"And the Philistines seized him and gouged out his eyes, and brought him down to Gaza, and bound him with bronze fetters; and he ground at the mill in the prison."
The Holy Bible, Judges 16:21

Gaza City in August can be inordinately hot with temperatures reaching the high 90's. The cab ride to the Holy Family Church was stifling, as the cab had no air-conditioning, but Father William was not phased. In fact, the heat of the day felt reinvigorating, loosening his muscles, and relieving the pent-up emotions and tension from his month-long sojourn in Rome. It was a new sojourn now, a spiritual undertaking to rescue an innocent soul from whatever was haunting her, an innocent soul who saw visions.

The Vicar, Father Stephen, was waiting for him when he arrived. He was a small and thin man with a withered appearance, appearing as if he had spent the majority of his seventy or so odd years in a harsh desert climate.

"Welcome, Father William," he said in a rather high-pitched and squeaky voice, his hand out-stretched, and a faint smile on his aged face.

Father William took his feeble hand and shook it gently in order not to break it into a hundred pieces.

"I'm excited to be here, Father," he said. "And, most importantly, to help the young woman."

"Yes, Father, it will be a delicate undertaking. As you know, she is blind but her other faculties are as sharp as a shepherd's knife. Now then, Sister Sophia will show you to your quarters, which are located directly behind the church, after which we will have lunch and speak of the young woman."

"And of her visions, Father?" asked Father William.

"Especially of her visions. Now, please, follow Sister Sophia."

As Sister Sophia pointed to the church, not saying a word, Father William followed closely behind her carrying his two suitcases.

"Sister," he said. "What is your order, if I may ask?"

The nun stopped and turned abruptly around. She ran her long and slender finger across her paper-thin lips, as if to seal them, and then she shook her head as if to say no. She then removed a small discolored rosary, old and tarnished, from her black cassock, which dragged along the ground. She held the rosary up to eye-level, again placing her finger over her lips.

"Ah, you are a member of the Rosary Sisters who run the clinic," said Father William.

The nun nodded, a glimmer of a smile forming on her hoary face.

"Well, then you must be acquainted with Serapia, the young blind girl who sees visions. She works at the clinic," said Father William.

A grim expression suddenly appeared on the old nun's face. Her dark eyes narrowed, almost in a sinister manner, and her brow became inordinately wrinkled. She deftly put her rosary back into her pocket and, without saying a word, pointed to the church and resumed her slow gait toward it.

Chapter 2

*"For still the vision awaits its time; it hastens
to the end – it will not lie. If it seems slow, wait
for it; it will surely come, it will not delay."*
The Holy Bible, The Book Habakkuk, 2:3

It was just the two of them sitting in the small dining area of the rectory. Father Stephen broached the subject of Serapia first.

"You know, Father William, it is a delicate situation. There are only a few of us here who know about her special talents, shall we say."

"Special talents, she sees visions, Father. I don't know if I would characterize that as a talent or as an ailment," said Father William, between bites of his meager lunch.

"Yes, it is a dilemma of sorts, Father," said the Vicar.

"And Sister Sophia, does she know, as well?"

"Yes, I believe that you have learned that from your short time with her."

"I also learned that she is a mute, Father," said Father William. "But there is more to her story, am I not correct?"

"There is more to everyone's story, Father William, even yours. Time will dictate when, and if, those stories will be told, hmmm?"

"I see," said Father William.

"Now you have been sent here, more or less, to monitor the situation and to determine if there is a solution to the young girl's, shall we say, affliction and then, hopefully, apply that solution to the matter at hand. After all, you were present when the young boy died in the sacristy, the young boy who lived with Serapia."

"Lived with her?" asked Father William.

"Yes, didn't you know? Serapia is an orphan and was a foster child living with the boy and his parents. It seems that after the boy died, apparently from an epileptic seizure, at least that's what the medical records indicate, the fate of Serapia was sealed, the foster parents simply holding it against her, for whatever reason we may never know. Then, however, that all became moot as the boy's parents were involved in a horrific car accident, both of their bodies being severed in half and, well, the rest of the story remains here with the young girl."

"But the dead boy said she saw visions, whatever that means. I was there. I saw his eyes roll up into the back of his head. I saw him choke on his tongue. Visions, Father Stephen? Yes, visions, I believe, are at the bottom of all of this," said Father William.

"Perhaps the deaths of the boy's parents were related to those very same visions but, then again, perhaps not. That is why you are here, Father, to solve that intriguing riddle and, hopefully, rescue a young soul from the Abyss. Well then, as soon as your lunch is concluded, perhaps we can take a short walk to the clinic and I will introduce you to the young woman and then, as you said, we can begin our journey to getting to the bottom of all of this because, Father William, there is a bottom and there are many unanswered questions that need to be addressed."

"One other thing, Father," said the young priest. "Why here? Why to Gaza City was the young girl sent?" asked Father William.

"That question you will have to ask Sister Sophia," said the Vicar, an unholy expression birthing on his otherwise bland face.

"Sister Sophia?" asked the young priest. "But she can't speak."

"Yes, but she visions, Father William. She also sees visions."

Chapter 3

"She was beheaded, Father. Yes, my namesake was beheaded for her faith in our Savior," said Serapia, a simple expression on her face not belying any semblance of regret.

It was just the young priest and the young girl who saw visions who were now seated alone in a small room in the back of the clinic where she ministered to the weak and feeble, both of body and of mind. They were seated across from each other on the plain of good and evil in that barren and desolate place known as the Wasteland, a bare and wooden table the only tangible barrier between them, but there were certainly other barriers to bridge.

"Yes, Serapia, there are several beheadings mentioned in the Bible," said the priest. "The Apostle John the Baptist was beheaded, as was his brother James. David defeated Goliath, a giant, killing him and cutting off his head. Revelations speaks of it, as well."

"Oh, but my name is not mentioned in any parable, nor in any psalm, nor in any biblical verse but, yes, beheadings, if not commonplace, did occur," she said. "But not of a woman."

Her eyes were shut tightly, yet the priest felt that they were searching his soul for answers. He thought hard, struggling with what mysteries were held behind the curtain of where those silent eyes dwelled.

"Not of a woman, specifically, Serapia, but Revelations deals with man and woman," said the priest.

"That is so but that is vague, Father. Yet it seems that somehow I have assimilated the emotions from those atrocities, those beheadings, into my very soul and they, on occasion, transmute themselves into visions, some holy and, unfortunately, some equally not as holy, dear Father, and now I implore you, I beseech you in no uncertain terms to aid me in ridding myself of such unwanted thoughts and dreams."

"I am here to help you, Serapia," humbly said the priest, taking her small hand in his, which felt inordinately cold. "That is why I have come."

"The psychologists and psychiatrists were unable to help me," she said softly, tears beginning to form where once vibrant eyes dwelled. "The social workers failed, as well. So how is it that you, a simple priest and not even a skilled exorcist, will be able to help me, dear Father?"

She then slowly opened her eyelids and the priest had to catch himself from gasping in fright. Two orbs as white as hen's eggs and as large as tarnished nickels stared back at him, reflecting no light and giving no quarter, and seeming to be afloat in a discolored off-white prism of their own making. The priest regained his composure quickly because to do otherwise, he feared, would result in a lost soul drawing even further inward to the confines of her self-doubt.

"Serapia, psychology was my major in college and being an ordained priest and skilled in interpreting Biblical scripture, well, I feel as if my concept of holiness is intact because holiness in all of this is our ally. That is what I bring to the battle, my arsenal so to speak, Serapia, to thwart whatever demons are haunting you if, in fact, there are such demons."

"Demons, yes, Father, be assured of that! But are you trained in deciphering symbolism and in interpreting dreams and so-called night visions, in quantifying holiness in no uncertain terms, in balancing good and evil on a delicate pendulum that can sway one way or the other based upon one's morality, or lack thereof? Are you skilled in casting unholiness to the depths of wherever lost souls dwell? Do you understand the subtle psychology of the inner mind where these thoughts manifest themselves and where they are birthed and eventually spewed forth like unwanted corrupt incursions? Can you help me, dear Father, because if you cannot, I surely must die?" she asked in a voice devoid of even a sliver of hope, a voice that faded away into nothingness.

Chapter 4

"Charm is deceitful, and beauty is vain, but a woman who fears the Lord is to be praised."
The Holy Bible, Proverbs 31:30

The priest did not sleep well that night, his first night at the Holy Family Church. He seemed to be constantly dreaming but not about anything in particular and when he finally awoke in the morning he could not remember a damn thing about what he had dreamt. His eyes were glassy and red, as if he had been rubbing them all night, his mouth as dry as wind-blown hay, and he was as stiff as an old board.

The sun was just rising, its incipient rays creeping through the tired shades on his window. He glanced at his watch that was still on his wrist, having forgotten to remove it the night before – 8:00 a.m. His morning appointment with Serapia would be within the hour. He shook the cobwebs from his head and convinced himself that a breakthrough, no matter how minor, would take place today. He would chip away at her outer façade of distrust and, hopefully, resurrect a meaning to that which lay at the heart of her troubles.

Soon they were seated in the same room and at the same table as the day before, a lukewarm cup of coffee on the table in front of the priest and neatly folded hands on the same table opposite of where he sat.

"Your eyes, Father, they are quite red," Serapia said. "Have you been up all night?"

"I slept poorly, child, but I simply can't remember about what I dreamt if, in fact, I dreamt at all," said the priest.

"Oh, but I dreamt about you, dear Father. Have you been to Rome recently?" she asked, her eyes tightly shut.

Rome? It was like a dagger striking the priest's fast-beating heart. He now succinctly understood that this was going to be no ordinary undertaking where a sprinkling of holy water here and there, and a Hail Mary or two said, would solve the mystery that was afflicting this lost soul.

"Yes, I have been to Rome and not too long ago," said the priest.

"Father, do you know anything about my namesake, Serapia?" she asked.

The priest did know a few things. He had researched it before coming to Gaza.

"Well, she was canonized a Roman saint. She was a slave and a martyr," said the priest. "She was born in Antioch in ancient Syria in the late 1st Century to Christian parents who were being persecuted for their religious beliefs and who eventually fled to Rome," said the priest.

"Yes, dear Father, she was a slave, as well, just as I am a slave to these visions that haunt me. Do you think there is a connection here, spiritual or otherwise?" she asked, her hands now unfolded and laying face-down on the table, as if willing it to rise.

"Well, there is a similarity, I believe. Saint Serapia, at the age of marriage, and you, my dear, are nearing that milestone, sold all of her worldly possessions and gave them to the poor."

"I will be 17 in a month, Father, but I have no worldly possessions. Father William, I am as poor as a church mouse," she said.

"But you are giving yourself, mind and soul, to the poor and the needy in your daily work here with the Church," the priest said.

The young girl neatly folded her hands and lay them on the table again as before.

"Yes, Father, she was the slave of a Roman noblewoman named Sabina, who later became a saint, as well," she said. "Have you heard of Saint Sabina?" she asked.

The basilica of Santa Sabina in Rome, the wooden doors of which were implanted deeply in the recesses of his very soul, of course, he had heard of it, and he would never forget it, nor would he forget the reason why he had been found kneeling and crying uncontrollably at that holy place by Father Morrison. He would never forget his own soul-searching that took place at those holy gates in order to understand the dichotomy of lost love and holiness.

"Yes, I have been there," said the priest calmly.

"And the wooden doors, did you touch them, Father? Did you lay your hands upon them and run your hands across the wooden panels of the crucifixion? Did you experience their holiness?" she asked.

"Yes, I did," said the priest, almost in a whisper.

"You see, Father, that is a holy place. Sabina, later Saint Sabina, was so influenced by my namesake and her charitable deeds and piety that she became a Christian, as well, and when Serapia refused to worship false gods they attempted to set her on fire, and when that didn't work, she was beheaded by a sword," she said, crying dry tears. "Then Sabina was accused of being a Christian and was also martyred."

The priest was on the verge of crying himself, seeing the young and innocent soul so distraught.

"Serapia's body is buried near the Vindican fields in Rome next to Sabina's tomb, Father," she said. "And Sabina's relics eventually found a resting place at the basilica Santa Sabina. This church is dedicated to both Sabina and Serapia. That is why it is such a holy place, Father, and you have experienced that holiness."

Experienced it? Wept uncontrollably while on his knees would be a better way to put it but, yes, he had experienced that innate holiness.

"And so, Father, the wooden doors of Saint Sabina, I dreamt about them last night. I dreamt that you were kneeling in front of them, crying uncontrollably, and running your hands across the panels of the crucifixion and I dreamt that you found the meaning of holiness," she said. "And I then dreamt of the Aventine Keyhole and of a young woman, and I also felt that, through her, you had found the meaning of not only holiness, but of true and unremitting love, as well, and her name was Leonora. I felt that although she possessed beauty and charm, that she feared the Lord, as you do, Father, but the Aventine Keyhole in Rome, Father William, have you looked through it?"

Looked through it? Fell in love while doing so would be more *apropos*.

"Yes, my dear, I have," said the priest.

"You do fear the Lord, don't you, Father?" she then solemnly asked.

At this juncture in time the priest was in a quandary as to what he feared more, the Lord his Savior or the visions from the namesake of a beheaded saint.

Chapter 5

"When the unclean spirit has gone out of
a person, it passes through waterless places
seeking rest, but it finds none."
The Holy Bible, Matthew 12:43

It seemed like it was always morning and it seemed like
he was always distraught. Again, the priest did not sleep well
during the night. Images of Sister Sophia kept popping in and
out of his head. She was a sad-eyed woman with dull gray
eyes that appeared like dusty smoke and within a short time
he would be sitting with her and with Serapia at that same
wooden table and discussing the meaning and source of the
visions that haunted both of them.

His dreams from the night before, if dreams they were,
were as jumbled as a deck of playing cards scattered across a
poker table. He simply could not remember a thing. Maybe
that was good but in the back of his mind he knew that within
a few short minutes Serapia would be describing a vision that
she had seen and that was the cause of the priest's sleepless
night, albeit his recollection of those events was as tight-lipped
as Sister Sophia's silent mouth.

Soon two pairs of eyes met on the plain of good and evil
while the silent orbs of an afflicted young woman, eyeless in

Gaza, hid behind a mysterious curtain of uncertainty. The atmosphere was thick with anticipation as Serapia and Sister Sophia communicated through sign language and then Serapia spoke first.

"Sister Sophia saw a vision last evening, Father William. She wants to tell you about it. I will communicate with her in sign language and then I will tell you what she saw," said Serapia.

The priest looked at Sister Sophia whose hands covered her face, as if she were conjuring up the intricacies of the vision she had seen. She then sat stiffly upright, her hands now in the air and communicating her message to Serapia.

"She says, Father, that she dreamed about you last night. The dream was most disturbing and she cautions you to stop at this point. You may not understand the interpretation of her vision."

The priest sucked in a deep breath, his heart beginning to beat a little faster. He had come to Gaza to save a young woman and now it seemed as if he was the one who required saving.

"I am a strong person who has recovered the sense of holiness I once lost," said Father William. "If it is about that, then proceed."

Sister Sophia signaled again with old and gnarly hands to Serapia, her eyes narrowed and her lips motionless.

"Yes, it is about holiness, Father William, your holiness and, most assuredly, about your future," said Serapia.

"Then begin," solemnly said the priest, seemingly consigned to his ill-fated future.

The hand-waving from the aged nun began again in earnest, the young woman opposite her appearing as inert as a block of granite, her facial expression blank, her eyelids tightly closed and then she spoke.

"She saw your head in the lunette of a guillotine, Father. You were dressed in a black cassock and wearing a white collar. She saw a young woman with her hands upon the rope as the moutons crashed down and as the blade struck your neck. The young woman then picked up your head and held it in her hands," Serapia said.

The priest expected something malevolent, something gruesome, but this was beyond the pale. Was it, however, just a premonition of how he was to die at some preordained point in the future, or possibly at some unanointed time, perhaps in a car accident where his head would be severed?

"There is more," said Serapia. "Should I continue?"

The priest' hands were clenched tightly under the table, his knuckles were as white as freshly fallen snow.

"Please, Serapia, have her finish her story because, perhaps, that is what it is, only a story," said Father William.

"She says that the young woman who is holding your head in her hands is standing next to you and offering it to you, Father, and that you are not dressed in a priestly fashion. You simply appear as a young man and then all goes black."

The old nun then suddenly collapsed onto the table, appearing as if an unclean spirit has exited her body. Serapia quickly went to her rescue, lifting up her head.

"She is still breathing, Father. Please, help me take her to the infirmary."

Chapter 6

6 Months Later

**"But as he who called you is holy, be holy
yourselves in all your conduct; since it is
written – You shall be holy, for I am holy."**
The Holy Bible, 1 Peter 1:15

The priest sat across from the good Monsignor, his eyes slightly grayer than before but certainly not as gray as the eyes of Sister Sophia.

"It is good to have you back, Father William. Father Stephen said you were quite successful, notwithstanding the fact that one of their devout nuns died during your visit but unfortunate things do happen, don't they?"

They do, indeed, thought the priest. His thoughts and prayers were with Sister Sophia who died shortly after divulging her vision to him.

"Yes, it was unfortunate, yet she appeared content when she passed and that is a good thing, Monsignor."

"And tell me of your success with Serapia, the young woman," said the Monsignor.

"We spoke daily, Monsignor," said the priest. "And when I left I detected a certain degree of holiness in her attitude, in her smile, in her daily bearing upon things, and in her passion to help others that was not apparent when we first met. Like her namesake, Monsignor, I believe she is on her way to sainthood, as well, and that she has reshaped the visions that come to her in a positive fashion. Possibly the death of the nun exacerbated that change, possibly not, but the fact remains, she is quite a different and better person from when I first encountered her.

"So you were successful with the young woman. That is good. Now were you successful with yourself, Father William?"

"Yes, Father, quite successful," said the priest, removing his white collar and placing it succinctly in front of the good Monsignor on his desk. "I am leaving the priesthood. I have rediscovered my holiness and I will not lose it again."

"I feared as much," said the Monsignor, seeming to be not at all distressed by the priest's remarks. "And what will you do, William?"

"Hopefully, I will remain holy in all of my conduct," said the now ex-priest. "And, hopefully, I will fall in love."

"Yes," said the Monsignor. "But falling in love is one thing, while being in love with someone who is also in love with you is an altogether different matter."

Epilogue

In the Wasteland things are simply unpredictable. Take the simple concept of holiness, for example. Some people are imbued with that unquantifiable quality, while others simply are not. Ordinary people can espouse that virtue, as well. Further, one does not have to be a religious cleric or zealot to have it. Many of those curious individuals have strayed from the tenets of the Church by committing ignoble and repulsive acts, their souls, if souls they have, forever cast into the bottomless pit.

So as our protagonist in this saga, William, formerly Father William, having come to grips with his personal concept of holiness, and morality for that matter, as well, sits at the roulette wheel in Vegas as, in his own words, just an ordinary guy, and deciding whether to place his bet on red or black, he is content with himself and his choice to leave the priesthood. Along the path to this decision he had discovered true love, albeit devolved from only a single, solitary kiss on the cheek, it, nonetheless, remains imprinted in his soul.

Ah, dear reader, and what of the young woman who retrieved his severed head from the basket, you ask? Well, surely that young woman was not Serapia, her namesake having been beheaded herself. I am sure you agree with me on that point. Well, that leaves us with the enigmatic Leonora.

Surely, having released the moutons resulting in the blade descending upon the priest's neck, well, that act, in essence, did not kill William, it only killed the vocation with which he struggled on a daily basis because, you see, he simply wanted to fall in love.

So, as he places his bet on red, Serapia's words continue to run through the back of his mind. *"Just as you rediscovered holiness, Father, you will rediscover true love."* After all she sees visions.

And as that bouncing red demon of chance careens along the roulette wheel, eventually resting on who knows where, there is a slight tap on the former priest's shoulder, followed by a sweet voice that triggers pent-up emotions to pour over his broken dam of lost love. For it is here that he turns around and she is standing there, her deep-set violet eyes penetrating and riveting his very soul, her hair, not as long as before, yet cascading along her bare shoulders and inviting him to live there.

"Father William?" she incredulously asks, a tray of cocktails held in her hands, her tight-fitting and lowcut Playboy Bunny outfit pink and flirtatious, her eyes in unison dancing the Salsa.

The former priest only smiles, the Aventine Keyhole, the wooden doors of Saint Sabina and the small missive instantly implanted in his midbrain like a star exploding, and then that single, solitary kiss races to the finish line of his memories. *"Just as you rediscovered holiness, Father, you will rediscover true love."*

"Just call me, William, Leonora."

And as for the future of Serapia, all is well. After all, she still sees visions.

The Coffee House
and Mrs. Brown

Chapter 1

God I hate it when I spill coffee all over my jacket. I was exiting the coffee house and somehow the lid came off of my cup. I reached down to pick it up and there she was, standing just outside of the door and trying to get her car keys out of her pocket while holding a bag of something or other in her free hand, along with a plastic cup of coffee, I imagined. I succinctly came to her rescue. I was a boy scout as a kid and I guess that *good deed for day* just stuck with me.

"Here, let me help you, ma'am," I said, catching her cup of coffee just as she lost her grip on it.

"Oh, thank you so much," she said. "You are quite the gentleman."

I've been called a lot of things in life but gentleman, well, that was kind of at the bottom of the totem pole of compliments.

"You're welcome. I always like to help out a lady in distress," I said.

She was driving a late model snazzy Jaguar, a deep blue color, almost purple, but then I thought for a moment, they don't make purple cars, do they? Anyway, her license plates read *MEOW*. I surmised that she was either a cat lover or a dog hater but, then again, there could be an inner hidden meaning there. She was now comfortably seated behind the wheel.

"I like your hair," she said. "It's so distinguished-looking. I just love a man with silver hair. I just want to run my hands through it."

Mercy! We weren't even on our first date.

"You can call me Loretta," she said, offering me her slender hand through the driver's side window.

I gently squeezed it, making sure not to shake it like a longshoreman. I just hate shaking hands with women. Anyway, it felt quite soft, her hand, that is, and her fingernail polish was quite alluring, as well, and matched her lipstick, a kind of a pink-purplish color.

"I like your lipstick," I said.

"It's fuchsia, like my fingernail polish," she said, wiggling her hands through the window. "But you haven't told me your name."

"I'm sorry, it's Frank," I sheepishly said, having been somewhat caught up in her more than intriguing machinations.

"Well, Frank, I'll bet all the girls call you the silver fox because of your wonderful hair, that is," she giggled.

"Girls? I'm 55-years old and retired, Loretta," I said.

"You know what I mean, Frank. Besides, I'm about your age anyway but since I've never worked anywhere, well, I guess I can never be retired but I really do like your hair."

"Well, it used to be jet black and as dark as octopus ink when I was younger. Then it turned salt-and-pepperish and now it's, well, describing it as being silver is being rather diplomatic. Most people just say gray," I said. "I wish it had never changed. I liked it a lot better when it was as thick as bamboo shoots and as dark as coal."

"Well, Frank, that could be one of your wishes. Now then, everybody gets three wishes in life. What are your other two?" she playfully asked.

"I think our coffees are getting cold, Loretta. Would you like to go back inside and grab a seat?" I asked.

Within moments we were back inside of the coffee house and seated at a small table near the window. A waitress soon came by and asked if she could warm our coffees. She addressed Loretta as Mrs. Brown.

Uh-oh!

"So it appears that you are married, Loretta," I said.

"You are quite the detective, Frank," she said, awkwardly grinning. "By the way, is that your car out there?"

She pointed to where my car was parked, a late model Cadillac, 2-door, white in color.

"Yes, how did you know?"

"C'mon, Frank, the plates read *X COP* and you do look like an ex-cop, silver hair and all."

"Yeah, I guess the plates are a clue."

"Let's forget about that for the moment, shall we? Now then, we were talking about wishes. You have two left, hmm?"

Okay, why not play along with her? After all, her tight, red miniskirt was crawling up her legs as if somebody had yelled – *Your pants are on fire*!

"Okay, well, I wish I had a hairy chest like Joe Namath had when he predicted he was going to win the Super Bowl," I said.

"Meow!"

"I'll take that as a vote of confidence," I said.

"And what's the last one, Frank? Make it a good one," she said.

Having you straddle my face doing the cha-cha while wearing a thick red belt, red lipstick and matching stiletto high heels, and nothing else but a smile, while *I'd do anything for love* by Meatloaf was playing in the background.

"Oh, just sitting her with you and having a nice congenial conversation," I lied.

"You're so polite but really, Frank, you are quite the bullshitter. Anyway, wish number three is granted. I'll see you here tomorrow, same time same place."

"And then you'll tell me your three wishes?" I asked.

She didn't answer me but only teasingly waved goodbye. With that she was up and out of the door before I could even respond but then she ducked her head back in and whispered *meow.*

Chapter 2

As soon as I pulled my car into the parking spot I caught a glimpse of her seated near the window. She was applying lipstick to her face. God, I hoped it was red lipstick. All of those other colors are mere pretenders but red lipstick, well, that can just turn the joints in a guy's knees into mushy peanut butter, especially when it's being dabbed all over a sultry dame's lips and Loretta, well, she definitely fit the definition of a sultry dame. She also fit the definition of a lot of other things but more about that later. So right now, as I entered the coffee house, I was focused on her and her more than curious machinations. Seeing me enter through the front door, she looked up and smiled broadly and then began to wave frantically at me, as if she had just won the trifecta. Hell with the trifecta, I was going to buy a shitload of lottery tickets. She was wearing red lipstick.

"I really like red lipstick," I said as I seated myself across from her in a rather small booth.

"I wore it just for you," she said.

"Oh, you must be clairvoyant," I said.

"No, I don't believe in religion, Frank. Please, don't hold that against me," she purred.

Now I understood the meaning of her license plate. I also understood that her vocabulary needed some fine-tuning.

"Let's forget about religion for the moment, Loretta, shall we? Anything good on the menu?" I asked.

"Well, I am a light eater, Frank. I'm just thinking about coffee and toast. How about you?" she asked.

"I'm leaning toward an omelet. You know, something with a lot of green peppers, onions and bacon. Something really spicy and dicey," I said.

"I like spicy and dicey," she purred.

There it was again. I was getting kind of used to it, the purring, I mean, and coupled with red lipstick on perfectly botoxed lips, hers I'm talking about, and today it was a black miniskirt, extra tight and extra short, along with a rather low-cut blouse, well, spicy and dicey took on a whole different meaning.

"I am so glad you came, seeing that we only met yesterday. I wasn't sure if you would show up," she said.

"Whenever I promise a woman something I deliver," I said.

"Is that true of sex too?" she asked, her finger resting on her lower lip and doing something seductively that I rather liked.

"Well, sex is always an interesting subject, don't you think?" I asked, just to keep the dialogue flowing.

"It's my favorite subject. If they had taught that in high school I'm sure I would have got an *A*," she giggled. "I'm really good at necking and at other things."

"Other things?" I asked.

"You know, silly, orgasms," she said, a gleam in her eyes that could shatter wine glasses at 20 paces.

"Yours or mine?" I asked.

"Who's keeping score? And, by the way, did you know that a woman's orgasm is ten times more intense than a man's? Did you know that, Frank?" she playfully asked.

Mercy! How did we get on this topic? It was only our first date, if it was date at all. Oh, well, I guess the concept of spicy and dicey can lead to a lot of interesting conversations.

"Well, kind of," I said. "You know, I dated this one young lady a while back and we were in her bedroom and she was on the verge, if you get my drift."

"I like drifts, Frank," she said. "You know, like big snow drifts that just rise out of nowhere and are real hard and pointed, and then after it gets too hot and sticky, well, they just kind of shrink away. You know what I mean, don't you?" she seductively asked.

Yeah, I felt I was getting the drift, no pun intended.

"Sure, now where were we?" I asked.

"We were talking about women's orgasms and you were telling me about the young woman in the bedroom who was on the verge," she said.

"Right, well, anyway, she had two roommates, both young ladies about her age. They were in the front room giggling and playing Parcheesi, I think it was, and my date began to get quite boisterous, a lot of panting and moaning and stuff like that, you know, like in the movies, and then I got a little concerned. Well, she then began thrashing around, the bedsheets winding around her legs and mine too, and saying things pretty loud."

"What kind of things, Frank?" Loretta asked, while somehow her high heels were running up and down my legs under the table.

"Well, words to the effect of don't stop. Please, don't stop. Faster! Faster! Goddamnit, you bastard, don't ever stop!!! It was quite embarrassing, you know, with the roommates there and all," I said. "And, besides, she was scratching the bejesus out of my back."

"Did you stop, Frank?" she playfully asked, her legs crawling up mine like jungle vines.

"If I had, I wouldn't be alive today. She was quite a wild cat in bed, if you know what I mean," I said. "Do you remember the song by Steely Dan – *Do it again*? The lyrics describe a guy *loving a little wild one*. Well, she was definitely a little wild one."

"I'm only 5'6, Frank, if you haven't noticed. I could be a little wild one. Why don't we just forget about breakfast and go back to my place and put that song on? Unless, of course, you're famished."

Hell with being famished, my other appetite was perking up. She then looked at me with a pair of sultry green eyes, the color of polished emeralds, that could melt chipped ice in a bucket.

"Meow," she purred.

Mercy! My temperature was rising. My eyes were squinting and my tongue was caught on my tonsils somewhere half-way down my throat but I really hadn't brought the *Mrs. Brown* subject up. I guess I supposed that could be broached at our next encounter. Anyway, that's how it all began.

Chapter 3

Just for background I should go back a bit. I am a retired police detective and I have never been married. I just never got around to it. I guess the job got in the way, that and I saw too many of my contemporaries sacrificed on the altar of misguided love. Divorce can do that to a person. Anyway, my concern at the moment was not centered on misplaced love or marriages gone bad, it was focused on who was the mysterious Mr. Brown and was he going to emerge from behind a shower curtain, like in the movie *Psycho*, and succinctly implant an ice pick in my back? So I was determined to resolve that curious situation with the utmost expediency.

"So, Loretta, I'm concerned about this Mrs. Brown thing," I said.

I was seated on a couch with a bunch of fluffy pillows in her high-rise apartment, which was located not too distant from the coffee shop where we had auspiciously met.

"Oh, that? Don't be concerned. I divorced his sorry ass years ago. I think he's in Phoenix and remarried. Anyway, he's out of the picture. I just tell everybody that's my name just to keep the strange men away," she said.

"Does it work?" I asked, not able to think of anything else to say.

God, I hate it when I say stupid things.

"Well, you're not strange, are you, Frank?" she asked, an intriguing twinkle in her lovely eyes.

Strange? Nah. Inordinately horny all the time, yup!

"No, Loretta, I am just an average guy," I said.

"You are being way too modest, Frank. Guys, especially handsome ex-cops with silver hair like yours are certainly not average. Now where were we?" she asked, naughtily positioning herself next to me on the couch, her long and slender fingers running up and down my thighs.

"Well, I think you were going to tell me about your three wishes," I said.

"Well, the first one was granted. You're here and sitting next to me, Frank," she meowed.

"Is this our first date?" I asked.

God, I hate it when I ask stupid questions.

"If it is, Frank, then we can't kiss. Nobody kisses on a first date," she said, her fingers getting tangled in my chest hair.

Boy, why was I asking stupid questions? Probably because Loretta was throwing a monkey wrench into my hormonal system.

"Now if you want to kiss me, Frank, let's just pretend this is our second date, hmm," she purred.

Boy, she backed me into a corner with that remark but before I could respond, she was unbuttoning my shirt.

"Just checking to see if you lied about that Joe Namath thing," she playfully said. "Oooh, you lied!"

Well, I do have somewhat of a hairy chest but not like the bear rug Namath has.

"My second wish was just granted, Frank," she meowed, slightly more sensuous than before.

Her legs were now wrapped around mine. It reminded me a wrestling move I had mastered while on the high school wrestling team junior year.

"Is wrestling your favorite sport?" I asked.

"What?"

"Never mind," I said.

Boy, another stupid comment. I felt as if testosterone was dripping from my ears in buckets and making my brain wobbly. Maybe that was the problem.

"Are you being funny again, Frank? If you are, well, I like to be teased," she purred.

Teased? Mercy, I knew what was coming next but I asked the question anyway.

"Now then, Loretta, that leaves just one wish left. What is it?" I asked.

"Just follow me, Frank," she said, as she got up from the couch and sauntered toward the bedroom like Sophia Loren before the wrinkles had set in.

Whatever she was wearing was being removed and thrown about in random directions, like a stripper after the speed date had concluded. She stopped at the bedroom door totally naked and meowing. I interpreted that as a clue, so I removed my clothes, tripping over my shoes, hopping up and down on one leg out of my pants, getting my shirt caught on my neck, and then I slowly approached her.

"Oh, my, Frank, you read my mind," she purred, as her eyes were riveted on the area just below the line of demarcation that surrounded my waist.

From the expression on her face, and the sparkle in her dancing eyes the size of small watermelons, there was no doubt that wish number three had been granted.

"*Meeeeeeooooowww*!!!"

Epilogue

Well, dear reader, every account from the Wasteland does not have to revolve around murder and mayhem, and adultery and philandering, though most accounts do. Sometimes in that curious realm things just happen to take a fortuitous spin and work out for the protagonists involved. So presented in the present narrative is one of those singular and unique encounters between a silver-haired and retired ex-cop and a never retired and never employed, Jaguar-driving and mini-skirt wearing, and cat-loving, sultry damsel of distress. And all because of a rather innocent and unexpected event, an innocuous spilled cup of coffee, and now, wishes having been granted for the most part, it seems that our two protagonists are on their way to premarital bliss.

It is, however, for you to decide if Frank's third wish will be granted. After all he did dole out a white lie when first asked by Loretta. And whether or not Loretta will soon be dancing the cha-cha or the twist while straddling his face, or whether she will be wearing a tighter-than-tight miniskirt or just a smile, or whether *I'd do anything for love* by Meatloaf or *Do it again* by Steely Dan will be playing in the background, be assured, it is up to you, dear reader, to determine if Frank's real third wish will, for all intents and purposes, come to fruition.

Meow!

The Japanese Girl
on the Boat

Chapter 1

I really didn't know her name, not her real name anyway. That didn't seem important at the time. It was more about whom she appeared to be and how she carried herself and, more importantly, how she looked at me with her somewhat slanted and almond-colored eyes. She wasn't full-blooded Japanese. I could tell that simple fact from her eyes. In fact, I could tell a lot of things from her eyes. I wished to hell I could have told the future from looking into them.

Chapter 2

It was one of those dull and desultory mornings in Chicago in late October when boat owners were preparing their boats for the winter and I was one of them. Mine was a meager craft, simple but tight to the wind, a small sailboat to be exact but it fit my solitary and melancholy lifestyle and my innate need for privacy. Montrose Harbor at this time of the year was a beehive of activity, as Old Man Winter was looming over the horizon like the Grim Reaper with a sneer on his face and a pulsating grip on his instrument of death, and simply waiting to expend his unwelcomed assault of slashing sleet and heavy snow onto the hearty victims of another Chicago winter.

She deftly moved about the deck of the small yacht as if she knew every nick and cranny by name. Small yacht, hah! The damn thing dwarfed my tiny sailboat by leaps and bounds. It was like comparing an ant to an anteater but I had never observed a single solitary soul on its deck all season until today but there she was, comfortably seated in some type of expensive boat chair and I was inexplicably drawn to staring at her. Soon she was standing upright in the crisp and clean morning breeze, stretching her slender and naked arms over her head as if she were attempting to reach the ascending fireball appearing east over the lake. Then she slowly emerged from the back of the boat into full view like a dainty ballerina about to perform a pirouette to soothing music from *Swan Lake* and then, appearing to survey the placid waters of the gray-green lagoon like a sentry on duty, she somewhat stiffened in the cool breeze and apparently spotted me looking in her direction.

There was, however, a slight hesitation in her gaze, that microcosmic bend in the moment of inertia running through the sensory nerves from the back of her brain and that terminated in the neurons in her irises. It was that brief but distinct and sometimes hollow and callous trepidation that precedes each and every human decision to act, an involuntary pantomime that I had recognized over the thirty or so odd years that I had policed the mean streets of the City with Big Shoulders.

Time was frozen in a test-tube of human anticipation for no more than a millisecond as our eyes inauspiciously met on the plain of good and evil, halfway between heaven and hell, and teetering on the edge of the Abyss, the descent into which inevitably leads to unknown consequences. It was somewhere in that mysterious realm known as the Wasteland where final outcomes and the decisions that precede them hang in the balance waiting for variables to be reduced and for the equation of *what if* to be solved, that I hoped for some common and unknown passion to birth itself from those sparkling gems she called eyes and invite me into the confines of the privacy of her thoughts but those eyes of intrigue were quickly shut tight, as tight as my small sailboat driving into a westerly wind in late August, and just as quickly she abruptly turned away from me and disappeared into the bowels of the floating monstrosity that I wondered if she called her home.

Chapter 3

"So who was she?" asked the bartender.

It was one of those makeshift waterfront dives located near the marina where I kept my sailboat moored and where former cops hung out and I was one of them. Atmosphere, what there was of it, was surely lacking, as was the professional décor of the clientele. Street people and day people were commonly found meandering about looking for a free drink or a handout, whichever came first. My thoughts, however, were not focused on them. No, my idle musings were fixated on the Japanese girl on the boat, whomever she was. She had mysteriously invaded my every waking moment from the time I had first set my eyes on her. It was an uncanny and, at times, unnerving feeling that overtook me because I had the premonition that we would somehow meet later on down the road at some unforgiving place, and at an altogether inopportune time, and facing a confusing impasse that neither of us had anticipated.

Why I felt that way I couldn't quite put my finger on it. Perhaps it was just unkind fate waiting in the wings to unceremoniously birth itself as it typically does or perhaps it was the innate 6th sense of the police subculture with which I was imbued working its wonders on me. Perhaps it was none of that at all. Perhaps I was just a lonely and pathetic soul, a retired homicide cop in his late fifties without a hobby, except for sailing alone for hours on end with his thoughts hidden away and neatly secreted in the back of his mind. Perhaps because sailing kept me secluded at a safe distance from people I was now simply looking for a new outlet on which to unleash my pent-up emotions. Loneliness can do that to a guy, as succinctly evidenced by the relationship-battered countenance of one Bernie the bartender, who was now characteristically invading my personal space in his customary manner with his furrowed brow and his day-old beard the color of cold oatmeal, as he refilled my shot glass with an amber-colored inebriant the rundown dive had the audacity to refer to as Irish whiskey.

"So what's her name?" he asked again in his gravelly voice sounding of dump-trucks careening down inner-city alleyways.

I wished to hell I knew.

"Just a girl on a boat. I saw her in the harbor yesterday and I keep thinking about her," I said curtly, slowly sipping the bitter liquid pollutant.

Bernie glanced back toward the creaking sound of the front door opening, casually nodded and then slowly moved away, apparently distracted by another so-called patron who had unceremoniously stumbled into the tavern half-drunk.

Just a girl on a boat. Those curious words ran through my mind unabated like an untamed stallion on the loose waiting to be corralled and broken and then ridden to some unknown place. I looked at my watch – almost 8:00 a.m. Perhaps she would be sitting in her deck chair like yesterday. Perhaps I could catch a glimpse of her again.

Chapter 4

The metallic and dented gray gurney was being wrestled out of the rear of the yacht by two paramedics who were no bigger than junior high school kids, one male and one female. The female I didn't recognize but the male was well known to me. Working homicide cases in the inner city can imprint a lot of things in the gray matter of a guy's brain and at this very moment in time my memory surges were focused on the smallish male paramedic whom I knew by the name of Richie. So I casually moved forward toward the crime scene, adroitly moving through the yellow tape and hoping to gain some insight into the apparent mayhem that had undoubtedly taken place there.

"Not so fast," barked the uniformed police officer standing in front of the red crime scene tape that surrounded the pier in front of her yacht.

His voice was stiff in demeanor and stentorian to the point that the still air around us shrilled in reverberations of shattered glass. He was rather tall and stood statue-like, as if his shoes were screwed into the wooden planking of the pier, but just then Richie jerked his head in my direction and, recognizing me, he yelled over his shoulder.

"It's okay, Johnnie. He's retired Homicide," he said, waving me forward in his direction.

The wooden-faced officer, appearing somewhat perplexed, relented and reluctantly lifted up the red crime scene tape that surrounded the curious spectacle of life and death. As I ducked underneath it and moved closer to Richie, who was now stiffly standing next to the gurney on which the unmistaken lump of a dead body rested, thoughts of somber, unsmiling faces and past homicide scenes that I had worked over the years eerily crept into my mind.

"Just one?" I asked.

"It's pretty much a clean crime scene, Sarge. Yeah, just one. It appears she hung herself," said Richie.

"Pretty little thing," chimed in the diminutive female paramedic at his side.

"Ah, this is Lucy," said Richie, introducing the petite and enthusiastic young paramedic to me.

Her miniature grin was plastered across her smallish face and she was just about to shake my hand when Compton appeared, red-faced and flustered, as usual.

"Thought you'd be having your breakfast of champions at some rundown bar near the waterfront by now," said Compton, spitting cop venom my way and then regarding his watch. "Somebody kick you off your bar stool?"

He was Detective Compton, Detective Fred Compton to be exact, and he was one of the reasons I was glad to have left the Homicide Division and taken an early retirement; otherwise, a screwdriver would have been inauspiciously discovered wedged between his beady and dull, mud-colored eyes in the middle of his misshapen and bent-in face.

"Right, Compton. So it seems you have the ticket on this one, eh?"

"Yeah, so what of it? What brings you down here at this hour anyway? Boating season's over. Somebody giving away free beer and pretzels? Thought you'd have a date with a bottle by now and I see that small piece of shit you call a sailboat is wrapped up tight like a sardine in a can," he said, looking toward where the *Maryanne* was moored.

"Yeah, right, Compton, all wrapped up. Just thought I'd come down and check on her one last time before the crane lifted her out of the water and put her to rest for the winter. So what about the body?" I asked.

"You an interested party or something? Maybe seen something you need to tell me about, hmm?"

"Just a girl on a boat yesterday. She looked Japanese, early twenties, I suppose," I said. "Never met her, really. Never even talked to her."

"Just your usual style, huh? Leering from a distance, as always?"

"You're funny, Compton. Sure wish I had that screwdriver handy."

"What?"

"Never mind," I said, approaching the gurney. "Mind if I take a look?"

My heart was beating like that of a panicked and crippled mare in a wild stampede with a bevy of ravenous wolves in hot pursuit. I then reached for the sheet of death that covered the corpse.

"Be my guest. Maybe you can give us a positive I.D.," said Compton, his rotted and yellow teeth protruding from his mouth like football pylons and appearing as if he were about to spit more cop venom my way but then his partner arrived, flat-footed and boisterous, and tipping over the applecart.

He was carrying a clipboard and assorted items of evidence in paper bags that had undoubtedly come from the crime scene inside of the cabin of the yacht.

"Hey, Sarge, how's retirement?" bellowed Brinkman.

He was Mortimer Brinkman but no one in their right mind called him Mortimer. The last guy that did is still trying to unscrew his twisted head from below his pushed-in neck and uncrack his knuckles that somehow buckled under their own weight when an ill-advised haymaker landed on good old Morty's face. That's what us guys who knew him called him anyway – Morty.

"Just fine, Morty. See you've been busy inside," I said, indicating the direction from where he came.

"Open and shut," Morty said. "Suicide, plain and simple."

Nothing was plain and simple about suicides. I knew that much from cataloging them for over thirty years but why get good old Morty upset? So I looked down at the corpse again. My hands were as cold as the iron bars of any holding cell of which I had ever been unfortunate to have been inside. I struggled to move my fingers but they felt like ice chips from some ancient glacier. I squeezed them together hard, just to get the blood flowing again and to get the color back into them, and then I slowly pulled the white sheet back from underneath where it appeared the head was positioned.

I froze for a moment, staring incredulously at the dead young woman, her innocent face claylike and grayish-blue, her eyes slightly slanted in that oriental sort of way that signaled intrigue was in the offing and her long and ink-black hair pushed to one side of her head, as if it were a pillow. The ligature, whatever it was, clothesline, old seaman's rope, a simple bedsheet, perhaps, had left its mark in raw skin. A deep laceration, reddish in color and upbraided on the edges in an ugly shape resembling braille, was visible on the side of her neck and looming vulgarly in front of me. It was a heartless scene but I had seen worse and yet it was still the portrait of a somber and expressionless face that held me in awe, as it always had. Her delicate eyes, somewhat half-opened, the distinct almond color still persistent even unto death, forced me to swallow hard and attempt to corral my emotions, as my throbbing heart nearly jumped out of my chest, as if being pulled by hot pincers.

"So, Sarge, you know her?" asked Morty.

Silence was a cruel companion as I stared deeply into her eyes but it was not her.

Chapter 5

I was regarding the *Maryanne* with quiet curiosity as the crane lifted her out of the water and onto the barge that would transport her to her temporary winter home. I was wondering if there would be a next boating season for me and if I would even be around and healthy enough to enjoy it. Life has that novel way of lumping up a guy's throat at times and buckling his knees when one thinks of the future, especially when one's future is as uncertain as mine certainly appeared to be, but uncertainty be damned, I suddenly felt a slight swirl of a breeze forming behind me, as if someone was approaching in determined but quiet steps. I turned around and there she was, curiously standing in front of me, her ink-black hair thick and glimmering in the sun. Her presence drew me in, her hair intriguing me and begging me to touch its silky texture as it waved in the cool breeze like an ensign on a rescue ship. It sensuously fluffed up against her slender shoulders that appeared perfectly symmetrical and appearing to defy the laws of chaos. It was her eyes though that held me in awe, almond-colored, wide open and dancing, and riveted into mine. They appeared uncommonly placid, appearing like cool waters rippling on a serene lake and then mirror-like, reflecting my startled image as she moved closer toward me.

"I saw you yesterday," she said, her voice even in tenor, yet subtle like that of a librarian whispering in the stacks. "I was wondering why you didn't come over to my boat and introduce yourself. I was waiting for you but you didn't come. You knew that, didn't you?"

Her words floated out of her imploring mouth and over her ruby-red lips in a sensual, yet refined, manner as if she were speaking with deep intent and profound clarity but with a hidden agenda. I could not speak. I tried and then I tried again but words would simply not birth themselves from within me. My lips were sealed shut and my voice was apparently lost in a bottomless pit.

"Didn't you?" she asked again, moving closer to me and nudging up against me, the warmth from her body all around me.

I could smell her fragrance. It appeared to be coming from the small white flowers that she clutched in her left hand. She raised them up to me and held them distinctly under my nose. I was just about to take a deep breath, to take in the full essence of their fragrance, to savor the moment for all eternity, when abruptly her right hand swept viciously across them and in front of me, knocking them away and onto the wooden planking of the pier. I looked down at them. The flowers had changed and now appeared to be black and lifeless, wilting and dead. I looked up at her and her eyes had changed, as well. They were now dark and sinister and held me motionless, appearing as if I were her prisoner and she were my keeper.

"Find me!" she shrieked. "Find me!"

And then all went black. I was alone in a room with no windows. The cold, dark and sinister walls were closing in on me and making me dizzy from their haphazard movement. I fell to my knees and frantically crawled on the damp and filth-covered floor to the door with no knob or window and pounded with all of my strength until my hands were bruised and bloody and dripping copper-colored rivulets of blood onto the floor. Then someone was squeezing my shoulders and shaking me and yelling something in my ear. Shaking me! Shaking me!

"Wake up!" yelled Bernie into my ear. "Wake up!"

And I did wake up, my face somewhat deformed from having been pushed into the rough and uneven surface of the bar in front of me, a graveyard of spent cigarettes and overturned shot glasses scattered about the only witnesses to my unfortunate demise.

"Better go home, chief," said Bernie. "Too much of that good old Irish whiskey can wreak havoc on a guy. Best to just go home and just crawl into bed and sleep it off."

I looked up at him. His eyes were hollow and dead, bartender eyes that had seen more than their fair share of human degeneracy over the years; stagnant and lonely eyes, and seemingly as desolate as the aching feeling that was birthing itself in what I feared was left of my soul.

Chapter 6

I didn't go home as Bernie had suggested. Instead, I went straight to the pier where the *Maryanne* had been docked and when I got there the mysterious Japanese girl on the boat was long gone. I knew that would be the case but I had gone there anyway hoping to get a glimpse of the girl who was haunting my every waking moment, hoping that she would have been milling about her yacht like before, hoping that I could talk to her. Just plain hoping. Damn it, in all of the confusion I simply had not noticed the name of the yacht. I suppose I was too focused on her and, never giving the name of her boat a second thought, I somehow had dismissed it from my mind but was it her boat at all or was she simply just a mere guest meandering about its deck, a custodian of sorts for some unknown agenda, someone who just happened to be at the wrong place at the wrong time? Nonetheless, the yacht was gone, as well as was the *Maryanne*, just two empty boat slips with gray-green sea swells lapping up against the waterlogged wooden pylons left in their wake and staring blankly up at me. As I looked into the murky and dead waters a plethora of unanswered questions appeared to be floating among the debris that bobbed up and down with the movements of the harbor and begging me to solve their mysteries. Then an uneven emptiness slowly began to form within me. *Find me!* How on earth could I find her? I knew nothing about her.

I rubbed my crusty and bloodshot eyes with rough hands. My thoughts were jumbled and misshapen and my head felt as if a thousand tramps were stamping their muddied hobo shoes onto my brain. Then slowly remembering, I reached into my pocket and retrieved a small and yellowed envelope. My boat slip renewal form for next season stared up at me. I felt a sudden gust of relief enter my forebrain. Maybe there was a solution.

His office wasn't far away. I looked at my watch. It was early afternoon. It appeared that I had been passed out at the tavern like a common drunk for most of the morning. I spit something bitter out of my mouth, phlegmy and as dark as old molasses, and into the slow-moving waters of the lagoon. It tasted of cheap whiskey and hollow despair riddled with more despair and then I wiped my mouth with the sleeve of my filthy flannel shirt like a common vagrant would do but these were just minor inconveniences. I cinched up my belt and tucked my tattered and stained shirt into my pants. Yes, perhaps the harbormaster could shed some light upon my precarious predicament. Perhaps he might know something about the Japanese girl on the boat.

Chapter 7

"Confidential, Sarge, you know that."

I did know that. I also knew that the pathetic excuse for a harbormaster who was presently seated in front of me owed me a favor, a big favor. So I just stared back at him, forcing him to look me square in the eyes and when he did I whispered under my breath the words *Mrs. Jenkins*. His eyes narrowed and he began desperately pulling at his shirt collar as if it were choking the daylights out him. His misshapen hands were now front and center on his desk, thumping out a cadence of fear and desperation to the tune of *Oh! Susanna*, and then he cleared his throat that sounded as if it contained a barge full of old coal.

"You wouldn't?" he said, more than asking. "It's confidential, Sarge. I can't do it. I could lose my job."

Confidential my ass. I kept staring at him but said nothing and then I pulled a pen from the cracked boatswain's cup that had his name vulgarly plastered across it in big red letters and which he had placed on his desk.

"The name of the yacht and who owns her, and everything else you know about it. A cancelled check or bank account would be extraordinarily nice," I said in a rather complacent tone, handing him the pen.

"Now, Sarge, c'mon, that stuff's confidential."

Didn't he just say that? This guy seemed to have a monopoly on the word confidential. Maybe he thought I was bluffing.

"The last time I checked, and I could be mistaken, Mr. Jenkins had a pair of fists the size of bowling pins. Wouldn't want those lethal meat hooks pounding on your scruffy little balls, would you? Screwing another man's wife when he's out of town and on his own yacht, to boot, makes for an uncomfortable scenario, hmm? Don't you agree?"

"Now, Sarge, didn't we have some type of agreement on that. I mean it was …"

I didn't let him finish. I held up my right hand and with my other hand I retrieved my cell phone from my pocket and began punching in numbers.

"Good old Charlie Jenkins, I'll just give him a call and see what he's up to. By the way, maybe old Mrs. Jenkins, Charlene was her name, wasn't it, maybe I'll just get her on the line too, just for old time's sake. Maybe she can bop right over here with her swiveling battleship hips and with her twin sentinels of lust bopping along with her. Maybe … oh, hi, Charlie."

The harbormaster, one Prentice Wainwright, Yale educated and schooled in all of the refinements that uppity dandies envy, a guy who'd never been more than fifty feet from shore in his life and couldn't tie a bowline hitch to save his ass, let alone spell it, was now frantically waving his puffy and girlie hands over his head and spastically nodding. I caustically smiled at him, the cop subculture reeking from my pores like hot gravy flowing over mashed potatoes, and then I held my hand over the phone.

"Do we have a deal?" I asked.

More frantic hand-waving and spastic nodding was in the works, accompanied by oodles of steamy sweat pouring forth from his furrowed brow. So I slowly removed my hand from the phone and resumed my conversation.

"Oh, nothing, Charlie. Now that the *Maryanne* is in dry-dock, I thought I'd just give you a call to see if you and your lovely honey, Charlene, would like to go out and have a bite some time. Sure, sure, sounds good Charlie. Sounds real damn good and I'll pass it along to Prentice, as well. Perhaps he might want to tag along for old time's sake, as well."

With that the conversation ended, as I pushed a legal-sized pad of paper towards Prentice that was lying on his desk.

"Now about that yacht," I said.

Chapter 8

It was a funny name for a boat, let alone an expensive yacht. I could hardly pronounce it. It seemed to be written in hieroglyphics – *PharomiamaZZZ*. It certainly didn't sound Japanese. Maybe it was a combination of words, possibly names. Anyway, more about that later, I thought, as I stood in front of the Continental Bank on North Water Street, a copy of the cashier's check Prentice had tersely provided to me neatly secreted in my briefcase. Hopefully, she could shed some light on the matter.

Her name was Louise and she looked like a Louise, mousy, pompous and as neat as a pin. She sat behind her desk as if she were an empress, her small and dainty hands bejeweled with sparkling and expensive gems and her smile nothing more than a straight line seemingly applied with a sharp stick dipped in ink. She appeared as if she were expecting an onslaught of problems, as her eyes were severe and followed me like the eyes of a jailer would follow an inmate walking on death row.

"Calling in a marker are you, Sarge?" she perfunctorily asked before I could even seat myself across from her.

She had a curious way of getting right to the point and dispensing with the unneeded pleasantries.

"Just one," I said, as I sunk down into the chair that seemed like more of a waterbed than a banker's chair.

"Hmm, then let's have it," she said.

She knew I was coming to see her. I had called first and I had spoken with her secretary, another malcontent whose voice was as stiff and uninviting as the look on Louise's sullen face; and who had all of the alluring attributes of a domesticated house cat, apathy, aloofness and self-absorption, but to refer to Louise as an old maid would be more than gracious. Anyway, I reached into my briefcase and retrieved the copy of the cashier's check that Prentice had reluctantly given to me and succinctly placed it on her desk directly in front of her and her rolling eyes.

"It's a cashier's check," she starkly remarked.

Damn straight, now we were getting somewhere.

"And?"

"And what?" she asked.

Let's go back a little, shall we? Let's go back to the time when I bailed Louise's stuffy and sorry sorority-born ass out of a bucketful of trouble. Maybe that had slipped her nefarious mind. A little reassuring information might help along the way.

"I'm calling in the marker about the silver ingots, the ones you seemed to have incorrectly inventoried and inadvertently placed in the wrong vault in the basement of the bank. Had to call the *G* in on that one before it was all smoothed out by yours truly. Chains of evidence can be so annoying at times, especially when dead bodies and silver ingots are concerned, don't you agree? Remember? Am I making myself clear, snookums?"

She hesitated for a moment. It was the type of hesitation that women exhibit when their too-tight underwear is running up the crack of their ass and they're deciding whether to reach down and pull it out, hoping that no one is watching, or the type of hesitation when they're caught in an otherwise defenseless position. I reasoned it was the latter.

"Oh, that. Yes, that handsome F.B.I. Agent was, well, so much more reassuring, and polite, than you were at the time," she sniffled under her breath. "Now, you were saying about the cashier's check?"

"Well, now that I have your undivided attention, it *is* drawn on your bank, so you should be able to tell me who or what entity was involved in its preparation," I said.

She pulled the cashier's check closer to her and adjusted her smallish reading glasses, the type that cloistered nuns wear in dark and gloomy convents.

"It is quite a tidy sum," she sniffled again. "For a boat slip, that is. Seems they paid for several years in advance. May I ask what this is all about?"

"Possible suicide on the yacht associated with it. It was docked in Montrose Harbor where I keep my sailboat?"

"Suicide?"

"A young girl, possibly of Japanese or Asian descent."

"Oh, my."

"Ring a bell?" I asked.

"Well, I believe, if I'm not mistaken, Eloise on the third floor handled the loan."

"Loan? This is a cashier's check for a boat slip," I said somewhat perplexed.

"Right, but Eloise handled the loan for the purchase of the yacht; that much I do remember. It had a funny name, the name that's on the boat slip that you've stapled to the cashier's check."

Bingo.

"Anything else?" I asked.

"Lots of tattoos."

"What?"

"The gentleman who negotiated the loan with Eloise had tattoos all over his arms, and very colorful, I might add."

"Japanese?"

"It appeared so."

"Well, then let's have a little chat with Eloise, shall we?"

"Alright, but don't mention anything about the ingots, please."

"Deal."

Chapter 9

"Are you with the police?" she asked.

"Not anymore. I gave it up. It was bad for my health," I said flippantly.

Louise rolled her eyes again in the way that uppity society tramps do when the champagne is too sweet.

"Well, then I don't see how I can be of any help to you. The matter is confidential. We simply don't give out information to private detectives without the proper documentation. Ever hear of a subpoena?" she said, her pointed nose turned upwards as if she had just smelled rancid meat.

Damn it, there it was again, that annoying word, confidential but, yes, as a matter of fact, I had heard of a subpoena. I had also heard of a left cross to the midsection followed by a right cross to the chin. I was pondering which one I would decide to address first.

"Look, Eloise, it is Eloise, isn't it?" I asked, giving her my best rendition of sad puppy dog eyes.

She didn't say anything but just flashed me a half-assed smile born of bored debutantes and worn out society snobs.

"Okay. I understand your position, legally, that is. And I was only …"

She interrupted me before I could finish the sentence. Reaching into her top desk drawer, she retrieved a business card and then rudely flipped it across her desk my way.

"The police have already been here, a Detective Compton, I believe. I told him everything I know," she said, nodding at the business card. "And by the way, he had the proper documentation with him, unlike you. I would suggest that you contact him for any further information. Now if you'll excuse me, I have to get back to work."

She was up in a flash from her desk chair, as if jettisoned from a downed fighter jet over the Pacific, and before I could look at the name on the card she was lickety-split out of the room. I glanced at Louise, more eye rolling. I looked down at the business card. Detective Fred Compton, CPD, Homicide Division, stared up at me. Maybe it wasn't as closed and shut as old Morty had intimated.

The cool air felt fresh on my raw face as Louise ushered me out of the bank building. I hadn't shaved in a few days. Maybe that's why Eloise had given me the brush so impolitely. Louise was now regarding me as an old mother hen would. I followed her eyes and I looked down at my shoes. A good polishing would do them wonders.

"Better stop drinking, Sarge," she said. "You are wearing socks of two different colors and your face looks like you've been mushing a dogsled in the Iditarod, and your shoes, do they still sell shoe polish?"

She had made her point. I got the message clear and unadulterated. She was right on point, as usual. So I tipped my hat, winked at her in my accustomed cop fashion when I had been succinctly taken to the woodshed, and was about to be on my way, but before I had taken a few steps she was rubbing up next to me like a lost lover and whispering in my ear.

"If it's more than just a suicide I'll do what I can for you but no wild goose chases, okay?"

I gave her a soft peck on the cheek and winked at her. Time to give old Morty a call and find out about the Japanese guy with the tattoos.

Chapter 10

"You calling in another marker, Sarge?" Morty asked.

"I didn't know I had a marker with you, Morty."

"You don't. So you're just asking for a favor from an old sidekick, is that it?"

That was it, plain and simple. Unfortunately, I didn't think Morty's previous description of the suicide was going to hold up in that same fashion.

"Sarge, are you just satisfying your pent-up curiosity or are you working off a binge? C'mon, level with me."

"Both," I said rather petulantly. "I don't think it's a suicide, Morty. I really don't. Something inside of me is just not sitting right. Seems your snot-nosed buddy, Compton, has been nosing around at the bank that had the note on the yacht. Know anything about that?"

"Close to the vest, Sarge? Promise me that."

"You can trust me, Morty. You know that."

The line went silent for a second or two, Morty apparently weighing consequences and potential bad outcomes on the seesaw of police accountability.

"We found some dope on the yacht," said Morty. "Meth, several kilos of the stuff. D.E.A.'s got the ticket now and Compton, well, he's kissing ass as usual and running down some leads for the Feds and right now they're in the process of seizing the boat, you know, civil forfeiture with the U.S. Attorney's office downtown and Compton is helping piece together the financial end."

"And the suicide?"

"Like I said, Sarge, open and shut. Just ask the guy over at the Medical Examiner's office. Tuney is his name, Frank Tunney, short guy, balding and on the back nine. Shouldn't be hard to find him."

"So that's it? It's a drug case now and you're out of it?"

"Yeah, got the girl I.D.'d. She was on a runaway list from Hawaii, the big island. In and out of drug rehab over the years, mostly meth. Half-Japanese, half-islander, she was only seventeen. Just a girl on a boat and probably servicing whoever came on board, know what I mean? Like I said, Sarge, it's a dead end."

"But she's not the girl I saw, Morty. There's another girl involved."

"Were you drinking when you saw her, Sarge? Were you drinking the night before? And the night before that? Booze can screw up a guy's metabolism and his memory. Maybe you saw what you think you saw and then again maybe you didn't. Hold your hand out in front of you, Sarge. Is it trembling or can you keep it straight? Open and shut, Sarge. Plain and simple. Gotta' go now and, Sarge, stop drinking and rejoin the human race."

"What about the guy with the tattoos?"

"What?"

"The front guy at the bank with the loan, know anything about him?"

"Better ask Compton, Sarge. He's running down that end."

The phone then went dead, as dead as my hopes of finding out who she really was. I held my hand out in front of me. For the life of me, I couldn't keep it level. It was trembling and my knuckles felt as if they were constricted in a vice. Maybe Morty was right. Maybe there really was only one girl on the boat and in my hazy and drunken state I had simply confused the issue but then again if there was another girl, in fact, whoever she was, she's either missing or dead. I tried to squeeze the thought of mistaken identity out of my mind. I tried to recreate the scene of the Japanese girl on the boat as I knew I had observed it. My memory was blurry and indistinct and coming back to me in bits and pieces, dripping in slow drops of gray-black snippets of images on blotter paper. It was like flipping through old black and white photos from days gone by. The images of what I was trying to reconstruct in my mind simply were flat and distorted, a graying film of confusion encompassing them. My head felt wobbly and my eyes were mushy. Maybe there was another way. I regrouped my thoughts and dug deeply into the crevices of my memory but nothing emerged. Then, like an epiphany, her name popped into my head out of nowhere like a glowing rescue flare in the middle of the night over turbulent seas. Maybe Maryanne could help.

Chapter 11

"You know I named my boat after you, don't you?" I asked.

"You never told me as much but from our past sessions, I kind of figured it out," she said, smiling in the way that neither portrayed her true feelings, nor gave the listener impetus to continue with the same line of dialogue.

Her name was Maryanne, Dr. Maryanne Turner, and she had helped me through some rather tough times in the past when I had skidded down the slippery slope of the Abyss and now I was hoping she could do it again.

"So why are you here, Sarge? It certainly isn't about the name on your sailboat. Has your drinking problem resurfaced again or is there another issue at hand?" she asked matter-of-factly.

I had cleaned myself up. I had shaved and I had even polished my shoes. My socks matched and I hadn't had a drink for well over several hours. I was hoping that my look of newfound respectability would spur her into action and so I got right to the point.

"It's about a girl. I just can't get her out of my mind. I saw something, at least I think I saw something, and it's driving me crazy."

"I'm a police psychologist, Sarge, not a marriage counselor. I don't know anything about speed dating and I don't run a dating service, remember? I deal with issues that are affecting police officers and their work performance, issues that affect their ability to get back on the job, not Romeo & Juliet issues. This issue that you have just presented to me is typically handled by outside professional help. Consulting with a private psychiatrist would be my advice and not someone who is employed by a police department, as I am. Besides, you're retired. Remember?"

I did remember that. I also remembered that she was the only person who had really helped me get through some rather oppressing times. That's why I was sitting here. Opening up to someone else just didn't appear to be a possibility.

"I trust you. That's why I'm here."

She sat stoically behind her desk, which was strewn with legal papers and police personnel files. She had the blank look of a cost accountant neatly painted across her face, as if there were a solution to every problem, and as if every problem could be summarily addressed by balancing personal ledgers of accountability against actions that had occurred, and often in the heat of the moment, and more often than not accruing undesirable outcomes.

"I'll pay you," I said. "Just like I would pay any other so-called professional you just mentioned. I know you can help me. I feel it in my bones."

"Last time, as I recall, we dealt with police performance issues, your fitness for duty and your self-inflicted drinking problem to be exact. Now you are asking me to counsel you on relationship-related issues, Sarge. Speed dating or whatever the hell you are referring to, well, that's out of my purview. It really has nothing to do with police work. Your problem seems to be kind of out in left field from what I do, if you follow me," she said.

"But it is about policing. In a way, it is. A girl committed suicide, or so they say, but I'm not convinced of it. I saw something else and that's what's bothering me."

"Were you drinking at the time, Sarge? Were your senses impaired?" she stiffly asked.

"Damn it, I know what I saw and I want you to help me see it again."

She hesitated for a moment and then keyed up her computer with her delicate and soft hands, a wedding ring conspicuously absent from the last time I had met with her several years ago.

"You're divorced?" I blurted out, immediately wanting to suck the words back into the bottom of my throat.

She looked down at her hands and then back into my eyes.

"I see there is still a detective in you," she calmly said. "Yes, it's been two years now. Has it really been that long since I've seen you?"

I just nodded slightly and then scratched my chin, wondering where the time had gone. She then resumed punching keys on her computer and when she apparently found for what she was looking, she scribbled something down on a small pad of paper next to her keyboard.

"It's been just a little over two years since our last session," she said.

"Well, it worked last time. I'm hoping it will work again," I said.

"There are no guarantees with hypnosis," she said. "It's a real crapshoot sometimes."

"Damn it, I know what I saw and you are going to help me see it again."

Chapter 12

"You've been under hypnosis before, so you should know what to expect," she said.

I did know what to expect. I expected to reenact the scene on the boat when the young Japanese girl stretched out her arms over her head and then curiously looked at me. I wanted to see it vividly, every image, every line on her face, every expression, every minute detail. I wanted to make sure that I was right; that the girl I had seen on the boat that day and the girl on that godforsaken gurney were not the same. That's what I expected. That's for what I was hoping.

"Now just ease yourself back into a comfortable position and follow the movements of the watch. Start to feel your muscles relaxing and close your eyes. Just follow the watch as it swings back and forth, back and forth, back and forth."

Her words drifted away from me into a cloud of nothingness, as I felt myself relaxing, slipping into a state of composure that could only be described as self-fulfilling. I anticipated a successful outcome and a relief of the stress that had been building up inside of me since the first time that I had laid my eyes on the Japanese girl on the boat. I felt the tautness in my muscles diminishing and my body becoming limp, as Maryanne's soft and calming words lingered in the still air surrounding me, back and forth, back and forth, back and forth. Christopher Cross' song *Sailing* was playing in the back of my mind.

My eyes were rhythmically following the shiny gold orb as I entered into a state of consciousness that felt eerily complacent but I wasn't unconscious to the world. I could hear, see and smell things. No pain, no fear, no depressive thoughts assaulted me, as an unearthly silence blanketed me like freshly fallen snow and now I was somewhat slumping into the chair, as the circular object moved back and forth, back and forth, back and forth, and in front of me like a slowly moving pendulum, and as her gentle and reassuring voice urged me deeper into a self-satisfying sleep. Deeper, deeper, deeper into a realm of which only I was an occupant.

"Sarge, can you tell me where you are?" she asked in her gentle voice. "Tell me what you see."

I looked around me. I was alone. No other person was visible, just the harbor and its assorted collection of watercraft, sailboats and yachts, and with the lonesome gray-green sea bobbing up and down. There was a slight breeze and it appeared to be early morning. I looked over my shoulder to the east and the sun hung slightly above the horizon, as if suspended by an invisible cord, its orangish-red glow appearing like the flame at the tip of a candle.

But then I looked back over my shoulder toward where her yacht was moored and I saw her. I saw her emerge from the back of the boat, from a deck chair in which it appeared she had been sitting. A lump the size of a small stone formed in my throat and I tried to yell to her but no sound was forthcoming, only the hollow silence of the deserted harbor remained.

"Tell me what you see, Sarge," said Maryanne. "Do you see anything?"

"It's her," I said. "It's her but she can't hear me."

"Is she alone?"

The unknown girl kept staring at me. I thought I detected a smile form across her face. Her ink-black hair, exactly as before, was gently waving in the soft morning breeze, and then she stretched her slender arms over her head, just as before when I had first seen her.

"I think she sees me," I said.

"What else do you see?"

She appeared ballerina-like in her movements. She was wearing a thin, black, see-through blouse, the kind that pampered women and concubines wear, and that appeared too light for the crisp autumn air. Perhaps she had been sleeping in it and had just emerged from the cabin of the boat for a breath of fresh morning air. Her pants were black, as well, sheer and possibly silk-like. Pajamas, yes, pajamas, she had been sleeping.

"She is wearing silk pajamas," I said.

"Look at her again, Sarge, and tell me what you see."

Her pajama bottoms were dragging along the deck of the ship as she moved toward the cabin. Looking away from me, her blouse was slowly rising up her back as she continued to stretch. Her back was now facing me and her skin was slightly exposed where her blouse had met her pants. As she moved about, her blouse rode up her back, exposing her smooth and somewhat olive-colored skin. Then I saw it. Just above her waist was a type of mark positioned centrally in the small of her back. I saw it! I saw it!

"I see it!" I blurted out, as if I had just found the Holy Grail.

"What do you see?" softly asked Maryanne.

"It's a tattoo. I think it's a tattoo, three large *Z's* in brightly colored yellow script running across the small of her back. It's beautiful. It fits her perfectly."

The beautiful brightly yellow-colored tattoo followed her movements rhythmically as she glided away from me toward the cabin of the yacht. It rose and then descended with each and every step she took. What did it mean, three Z's symmetrically placed on her back, as if by an artisan? Did her name begin with a Z?

"Can you see anyone else?" Maryanne asked. "Is anyone else there?"

Just as the unknown girl with the lovely tattoo was about to step into the cabin a dark figure appeared at the entrance that she was approaching, its back facing me. Then suddenly it turned my way and looked straight at me. It was another girl with long and wavy ink-black hair. Her face was somewhat hidden in the shadows and I strained to visualize it and then they both disappeared.

"There was someone else on that damn boat. Another girl but now they are both gone," I said.

I frantically looked from left to right and then back again. The sea swells had increased and the air was colder and whipping up around my face. I desperately strained to see her yacht but it was drifting away from me into the emerging white-gray morning fog.

"Do you see anything else?" Maryanne asked.

I did see something else. As the boat drifted away, starkly exposed on her stern was the yacht's name but I could only make out the last three letters, *ZZZ*.

Chapter 13

"What does it all mean?" I asked.

"In the long-run?" she asked.

In the long-run? What the hell did that mean? Was she viewing this as a damn football game? I hesitated for a moment. Did she think I was going crazy? Was she somewhat concerned about my mental health in the future and simply dismissing my present condition as resulting from lack of sleep and too much bad booze?

"The long-run?" I asked rather sullenly.

"Look, Sarge, I'm not doubting that you saw someone on that boat. I'm not doubting that at all. As far as your sincerity in all of this, that's pretty clear but …"

"But I saw two people and now one of them is dead and the other one is God only knows where."

"Okay, I'm with you on this one but I am concerned about your well-being. Please, trust me on this. I understand that in your mind getting this thing straight is paramount. Now if there were two girls on the boat, which is possible, then the other one must know something about the apparent suicide."

I eased back into my pre-hypnotic state. I looked deeply into her eyes; psychologist's eyes, sterile and non-committal, born from hours upon hours of peering into the souls of desperate patients. Maybe she believed me. Maybe she didn't but she was all I had at the present moment.

"I named my damn boat after you!" I blurted out. "Because I knew I could count on you. Can I count on you now?" I asked.

I must have caught her unawares. I must have hit a hidden nerve somewhere deep down in her subconscious where her soul dwelled because her face started to twitch a little where a smile sometimes forms. Perhaps no one had talked to her in those exact terms before. Perhaps no one had really counted on her when the chips were down and when it had actually mattered. Life is curious in that sort of way, two people encountering each other on the plain of good and evil in that quaint and uncompromising realm known as the Wasteland, where thought processes are somewhat real and somewhat unreal, and that's when a person let's their guard down and becomes vulnerable to suggestion. So I suggested.

"Help me find her. Help me find the missing girl. I fear that she is in danger. I feel it in my bones. My cop intuition is begging me to act," I said.

Chapter 14

Did I have her in my back pocket? I sure hoped I did. At least she had agreed to another session but undergoing hypnosis again was not on my mind, as I entered the austere-looking door of the Cook County Medical Examiner's office. My appointment was with the chief pathologist who had performed the autopsy on the dead girl found on the boat. His name was Dr. Frank Tuney and he uncannily fit the description Richie had previously given to me to a tee, short, balding and about my age.

I introduced myself and thanked him for agreeing to see me. He squinted slightly and his eyes caustically narrowed, and then he spoke with a rather high-pitched and squeaky voice.

"I'm just following orders," he said. "You must have some awful important connections upstairs, seeing that you are not on the police force anymore and really don't have a need to know."

A need to know? I grimaced inside but outwardly I smiled with my teeth showing. Yes, Maryanne had come through again for me by making a few phone calls and now the result was that a rather plump, out-of-shape and aging pathologist, who seemed to have lost his gym pass, and with eyes the color of muddy snow was staring at me and tapping his thick, unsharpened pencil on a stack of rumpled up papers that adorned his anything but tidy desk.

"Have it your way, Doctor," I said. "But, unfortunately, here I am and I would like to peruse the autopsy results."

"Peruse? Are you trying to impress me, Detective? Or should I say ex-detective?"

It appeared that the road ahead would assuredly have some bumps in it. Should I just gut-punch the sagging bucket of bloated flesh that sat in front of me and have it over with or should I bite my tongue, show my pearly whites, swallow my pride and sweet-talk his chubby ass? I gulped hard and down it went, whatever pride I had left, along with any wisecracks that would emanate from the police subculture that always lingered in the recesses of my mind at times like this. So sweet-talk it would be.

"It's just that I'd really like an opinion from an esteemed and well-known pathologist like yourself," I said with just the right amount of cowering sprinkled into the mix.

A glimmer of a smile crept out from the edges of his slit for a mouth and then his eyes lit up like flashing gumballs on a squad car in hot pursuit.

"Well, then let's have a look, shall we?"

He reached for a case file that was lying on his desk and opened it to a place that he apparently had paper-clipped.

"As I told Maryanne on the phone, and as I'll tell you now, the mode of death appears to be suicide, the manner of death is a knotted bedsheet wrapped around her neck and the cause of death is a broken neck and ruptured hyoid bone leading to asphyxiation. Have a look for yourself, Detective," he said smiling.

He seemed to have dropped the *ex*. Maybe he wasn't as inflexible as he appeared and perhaps he would change his opinion accordingly about the death. I reached for the case file that he had nudged my way and began to review it while he tinkered with an assortment of other odds and ends that cluttered his desk, as he whistled under his breath.

The photographs were crisp, clean and unnervingly severe-looking. Her neck had assuredly been broken. I could tell that from the way her head was awkwardly positioned in the makeshift noose. It almost defined a ninety-degree angle.

I flipped through page after page of the report and then something caught my eye under the section marked *Scars, Marks and Tattoos.*

"She had tattoos on the soles of her feet?" I incredulously asked.

"Yes, both feet. It appears to be a triple *Z, ZZZ*, on each foot. I haven't a clue what it means," he said.

"It's part of the name of the boat she died on," I said. "It had a strange name, *PharomiamaZZZ*," I said.

"Okay, well, maybe that makes some sense. She's been identified. Her name is Pharo Sato. Sato is a common Japanese name. Where the Pharo comes from, I have no clue. She appears to come from Hawaii, though, the big island. Detective Compton may be able to fill in the pieces for you. He's running down some leads relative to the Hawaiian angle with D.E.A., I think," he said.

The girl I saw under hypnosis had a *ZZZ* tattooed on the small of her back. Now the dead girl appeared to have the same tattoo but on the soles of her feet. Were they sisters? Or, worse yet, were they concubines or sex slaves, more or less branded with the mark of their captor? I was opting for the second choice but who was the mysterious sociopath whose calling card was *ZZZ*, and where was the Japanese girl on the boat?

"Detective, are you with me? You seem to be mumbling to yourself."

Chapter 15

It was several weeks later that I found myself in Honolulu and sitting in one of those trendy bars that align the beach of Waikiki. Eloise had done her best for me to track down who the owner of the death yacht was but had only come up with a series of blind trusts with non-existent beneficiaries, one after the other, that had eventually dead-ended with a bogus import-export company doing business out of Cambodia. Whoever owned the damn boat had done a yeoman's job in concealing his or her ownership interest in it. According to Compton, who had mellowed somewhat with respect to my interest in the matter, probably because I had cleaned myself up considerably, confided in me that D.E.A. had come to the same conclusion relative to the yacht's ownership.

So the only choice really left for me was to go to Hawaii and to see what I could find out. Compton gave me the name of a D.E.A. Agent working on the big island who I could use as a point of contact, if needed. So as the gentle evening breeze blew across my outdoor table, as I sipped a margarita on the rocks with plenty of salt, and as the Hulu dancers with their flaming torches and wiggling derrieres sashayed in the soft violet gloaming of the early evening, I waited for her to arrive.

For some odd reason I was caught up in the flaming torches of the Hulu dancers, somewhat hypnotized by the orangish-red glow of their flaming enchantment. I began wondering if this was all just a wild goose chase, a needle in haystack with an outcome as bleak as my checkbook. I was ostensibly trying to find an unknown, young Japanese woman who, on occasion, I wondered if actually existed, and in a Godforsaken place to which I had never been before. Then there was a soft tap on my shoulder and she seated herself across from me at the small table with flickering candles where I seemed to have daydreamed the afternoon away. Her name was Catalina, like the island, but as she told me, everybody just called her Cat.

"Sorry I'm late," she said. "Drug cases, had to tidy up a few things, you know what I mean. You must be Sarge. A least that's what they said you typically go by. I'm Cat."

She had a great tan but being stationed in Honolulu, who wouldn't? Her eyes were a sapphire blue color and her dark, wavy hair was just the right length, ending at her shoulders, which were bare. She was wearing a black halter top and matching black shorts, and black platform shoes with a rather high heel. Her legs were long and slender and I imagined she was either a swimmer or a runner, or possibly both. Her shoes made her look taller than she actually was but I imagined on the dance floor she would be a perfect fit for my 6'2" frame.

"Sarge, will be fine," I said. "And drug cases, well, that's kind of why I'm here," I said.

"Yeah, meth, right? And looking for a young woman, as well. Witness to a homicide or a suicide, wasn't it?" Cat asked.

"Just a Japanese girl on a boat I'm trying to identify. I don't know if she was a witness to anything. I really only saw her once and only from a distance. I don't know her name but I think it is Miama, or a variation thereof. Possibly it's her real name or maybe just a nickname but it was part of the name on the yacht where the other girl about her age was found dead."

"Still up in the air whether it was homicide or suicide, I imagine," she said.

"Exactly, that's why I'm here. As far as the dope, no offense, but for me that's just a sideshow," I said.

"No offense taken but that's why I'm here. Find the girl, find the meth connection, right?"

"Something like that," I said, as I clinked my glass to hers.

She had ordered something I couldn't pronounce. It had a mini pink parasol in it and several black olives, and it was a ruby red color which matched her lipstick. She didn't tell me but I imagined that she was about thirty years old. She had that look-but-don't-touch expression on her face and a certain toughness in her eyes that I surmised came from dealing with deadbeats and lowlifes on a daily basis. Being in the drug interdiction business can be unforgiving.

"I didn't know you D.E.A. gals could drink while on duty," I said.

"Who says I'm on duty? This is my day off and now they are playing a slow song that I really like. So let's dance, Sarge, and you can whisper in my ear everything you know about the girl you are trying to find. You know, get in the mood, loosen up a bit, just relax. This is Honolulu. It might help you remember," she said.

"Kind of like hypnosis?" I asked.

She looked into my eyes with a penetrating stare from deep glacier blue eyes.

"Nah, I save that for the second date."

Chapter 16

Sometimes you just hit it off with someone. Sometimes you don't. It's hard to explain. She wasn't what I was expecting. Maybe it was the pessimist in me but I was certainly glad that I was wrong.

"Well, Cat, you were right. I feel less tense and pent-up. Maybe we should do this more often," I said.

"Nice try, Sarge, but let me ask you a question. Why are you here?"

"Just trying to find a girl who is probably in trouble," I said.

"Sarge, there are a lot of girls in trouble. You could have stayed in Chicago and done that."

"Look, Cat, it's hard to explain. I'm not in love with her or anything like that. I only saw her once. Besides, she's way too young for me. It's just that something in the back of my mind is begging me to find her. It's probably the cop in me. Once you are ingrained with that mindset, well, it just won't go away and damn it, I am going to find her one way or the other," I said.

She smiled at me. I detected a glimmer of mischief in her eyes. She ordered me another margarita and one of those frilly girlie drinks with the pink parasol for herself that she had been drinking.

"I'm pretty good at reading people, Sarge," she said.

"Okay, so tell me about myself," I said.

She narrowed her lovely blue eyes a bit and smiled at me.

"So deep down inside who really are you? Well, you're just a guy who believes in unicorns, sad-eyed puppies and the end of the rainbow," she said.

"What about cotton candy and colored balloons?" I asked.

"That too," she said with a smile. "And that's why I am going to help you find her."

Chapter 17

We were seated at the same table when we first had met. Cat had spent the day checking out some thoughts about the case that I had provided to her. Now we were sipping the same frothy beverages as the evening before and the Hulu dancers were doing their thing with the flaming torches. She opened a small notepad she had taken from her purse and appeared to be studying it before she spoke.

"Well, Sarge, it seems you have won the trifecta?"

"How so?" I asked.

"Well, first we have an unidentified, young Japanese woman with tattoos on her back and then tattoos on the soles of the dead young woman from the yacht and, as you told me, there was an Asian guy, probably Japanese also, with tattoos, as well, who had something to do with the boat slip in Chicago, remember?"

"Lots of tattoos, yes, I remember," I said.

"Second, we have the drug angle, meth," she said.

"Okay, I follow you so far but what's the *tri* in trifecta?" I asked.

"The third variable is staring you right between your eyes, Sarge," she playfully said.

"Hulu dancers? I seem to have been focused on them and their curious gyrations," I laughingly said.

"Close, Sarge. Hawaii. We're in Hawaii," she said.

"And?"

"One plus one plus one equals the Yakuza. She's probably a girlfriend or concubine of one of those creeps, the guys whose bodies are imprinted with tattoos from toe to chin. You can't miss them. That's where we have to start, the Yakuza, plain and simple. That's where we'll find her and, Sarge, we will find her," she said.

Her eyes twinkled as if she had just won the lottery.

"Where do we start?" I asked.

"Where else? Find someone who knows what we want to know and who will give it up for a price," she said.

"Informants?"

"Right on, Sarge, he's one of them. I've had this guy in my back pocket for over a year. If he doesn't know where she is, she's not on the islands here."

"How soon?" I asked.

"I've set it up for tomorrow night. He's checking it out as we speak. I hope you brought a nice change of clothes because I imagine we'll be dining at some swanky high-end place tomorrow evening. That's their style, that is, if they're not partying on some expensive yacht offshore."

"Evening attire?" I asked.

"There are plenty of swanky shops along the beach. I'm sure you will find something appropriate and, please, dress un-cop-like, if you know what I mean," she said.

"You mean like a cost accountant?"

"Exactly, and get some tasseled loafers or trendy sandals. No cop shoes or shit-kicking alligator boots."

"Right," I said.

"Now, Sarge, they're playing that slow song I really like again. Shall we?" she asked, tenderly taking me by the arm as the violet gloaming of the evening crept in and thoughts of homicide and suicide momentarily dissipated from the back of my mind.

Chapter 18

I had never been to Hawaii before, only having seen it on TV and read about it in James Michener novels. Now, however, I was looking out of my hotel room at the beach at Waikiki and wondering where I should begin my search for the elusive Japanese girl on the boat. Would I find her window shopping at one of the upscale designer fashion stores that lined Kalakaua Avenue near my hotel? Or would she be sipping some exotic drink at the Kuhio Beach Hula Show under the twinkling moonlight? Perhaps she would be wandering among the plentiful waterside cocktail bars that lined the strip near the beach, or if she was as refined as she appeared to me to be, perhaps I would find her feeding a Komodo dragon at the Honolulu Zoo or whispering softly to the assorted collection of parrotfish and sea anemones at the Waikiki Aquarium. My mind was filled with possibilities, as I lay the tourist brochure down and again gazed out of the window onto Waikiki Beach. Perhaps she would simply be lounging in another yacht floating on the crystalline blue waters that defined the enclave of Honolulu.

Chapter 19

"The guy you are looking for is Zen Takagi," said the informant. "He is Yakuza."

He was a short guy with his arms fully tattooed from the wrist upwards. He was wearing a black short sleeve shirt, so I imagined the tattoos ran up to his shoulders. He had an open collar so I could see edges of the colorful body illustrations peeking out but his neck was clear and he was clean shaven. He was about 30 years old with no facial hair and he had a shaved head. He had a rigid appearance to his face and his rather wide-set black eyes were penetrating, to say the least. From what Cat had told me I imagined that his legs from the knees up were also tattooed with the colorful and circular flowery design I had observed on his arms but his loose-fitting black satin pants covered his legs. He wore dark sandals without socks but no tattoos were visible on his feet. Three fingers on his left hand were missing, as were two on his right. He stiffly introduced himself to me as Machii.

"So where can we find this guy, Zen?" I asked.

"He's easy to find," said Machii. "If …"

We were seated on a stiff wooden bench at the far end of a more or less deserted pier not too far from where the Hulu dancers were again plying their trade. The black waters of the harbor were as calm as if a thin sheet of ice covered their surface. Cat reached into her purse and handed Machii an envelope. He neatly tucked it into the lone pocket of his satin trousers. He then pointed down the beach at a wharf where a rather boisterous party was taking place.

"There," he said. "He is always a late arrival. He likes to make a scene. Two hours from now, I would think."

"And how will we know him?" asked Cat.

"He will be wearing all white, as he always does. You will see *ZZZ* tattooed on the back of his neck. That is your guy."

"Will he be alone?" I asked.

Machii had got up from the bench and was turning to leave. He looked back at the party and then he looked at me.

"She will be with him, the girl you are looking for. She is his girlfriend, his choice, not hers. Her name is Miama."

My heart skipped a beat. I read victory in Cat's eyes. I turned toward Machii who was walking briskly away.

"One other thing, does she speak English?" I asked.

"Yes, she speaks several languages but as far as Takagi, the only language he understands is pain."

He then disappeared into the blackness of the night, seeming to meld with it.

"You know, they cut off the tips of their fingers to, more or less, show affection for their superiors, their godfathers, so to speak," said Cat.

"Well, it seems that Machii has five godfathers," I said.

"Or just one demanding bastard," said Cat grinning.

"Right," I said.

"And all those tattoos?" I asked.

"Manhood, small penis complex, perhaps. Possibly pride in their perverted agenda," Cat said.

"Were you a psychology major?" I asked.

"Ph.D., mister, but don't let that intimidate you. You know more about these deviant types and their perverted antics and agendas than I ever could. Street time should never be underestimated in dealing with sociopaths," she said, her blue eyes dancing as if we were about to score a touchdown.

"Well then, shall we crash a party?" I asked.

Chapter 20

"Just one other thing, Cat," I said.

"Yes."

"I think we have forgotten something," I said.

"Like what?"

"A game plan."

"Oh, that? Don't worry. Cagney and Lacey will do just fine and Starsky and Hutch are in the perch with your sometimes friend and sidekick from Chicago, Compton. They'll be watching and filming everything. They'll bring in the cavalry, if needed," she said, indicating a second-floor hotel room caddy-corner from where the party was ongoing.

"Compton's here?"

"Well, he does have jurisdiction on the murder, doesn't he? If, in fact, it was a murder, that is," she said.

"And Cagney and Lacey, how will I recognize them?" I asked.

"Just look for a couple of lovely and alluring island girls with deep plunging necklines, sequined-spiked heels, and hundred dollar tans, and long silky black hair down to their shoulders. They should be easy to spot," she said. "Especially for a cop like you who doesn't miss things like that."

"Speaking of plunging necklines, Missy, I was a little hesitant to tell you but now that you've mentioned it, you look quite seductive tonight."

"I knew you'd like it, the cop in you, that is," she said, adjusting her low-cut black satin blouse which ended at her waistline and which melded neatly with her tight-fitting black leather pants.

She was part Hawaiian with deep, blue eyes that in the moonlight appeared dark and intriguing. Her skin had that island look to it, a soft and delicate brown that glistened in the sun and her hair was wavy and as dark as her eyes in soft moonlight and gently flowed across her shoulders.

"I like your leather pants, too," I said.

"I got them in the ass-hugging section. You don't think they are too tight, do you?" she asked whimsically.

"Nah, not a bit and now that we've got that straight, what about Starsky and Hutch? Do they look like Starsky and Hutch from T.V.? Is that why you call them that?" I asked.

"Their real names are Fetu and Haych and they look like small dump trucks. They are Samoans. Samoans and Hawaiians get along very well. They come in handy when you really need a roadblock but tonight they are here just in case things get out of hand. And remember, James …"

"James?" I interrupted her.

"Compton told me. I prefer calling you James. Sarge is too, well, cop-like, if you know what I mean. So remember, James, do exactly as I tell you. These Yakuza creeps are all about sex. Cagney and Lacey will lead off the festivities and then, hopefully, the girl can be separated from Zen and that's where you'll come in. Just grab her ass and get her the hell out of here. We'll take her to a safe house and Compton can get the rest of the story about the dead girl on the boat."

"And your people?" I asked.

"Well, the meth connection, of course. Now, James, I'm counting on two things. First, that she's desperate to get away from these bastards."

"And what's second?" I asked.

"That she will recognize you."

Chapter 21

"Do you think they'll card us?" I sarcastically asked, as we approached the boisterous party and a rather large and onerous-looking shit-kicker with deeply slanted dark eyes and a chin the size of a frying pan and full of scars, and whom I assumed was the designated leg-breaker for the evening.

"These Yakuza bastards, as I told you, James, are all about sex. They control the massage parlors that line Kalakaua Avenue in Waikiki, the topless and bottomless clubs, all of the porno book shops and movie houses, as well as the so-called Turkish baths on the islands. That doesn't even take into consideration all of the underage prostitutes they import into Honolulu."

"So that's the angle," I said, as the leg breaker began moving toward us.

"Right, I'll just wiggle my ass and then give him my business card with my cell phone number written on the back, along with a rather sultry peck on the cheek. In a heartbeat we'll be in and dancing the Hulu."

I just followed at Cat's coattails, not even glancing the leg breaker's way and we were soon mingling among the throng of partygoers. A few moments later she nodded toward where we had just entered.

"That's them," she whispered in my ear, as they jiggled their charms and whisked past the leg breaker, whose grin was as wide as his waistline.

Then across the crowded mélange of twisting and sweating bodies I recognized her instantly, the Japanese girl on the boat, who I now knew answered to the name Miama. She was dressed in all white, as was Zen who was holding her tightly by the arm, and then suddenly our eyes met on the plain of good and evil in that bizarre realm known as the Wasteland. It was only a snippet in time, a mere microsecond or two of reclaimed memories hidden behind our respective optic nerves, an outpouring of images, a waterfall of recollections, a spectrum where one instance in time held center stage, as she gazed into my eyes and as I gazed into hers, as the scene on the yacht in Montrose Harbor where we first had observed each other was recreated in all its unholy glory, and then the expression on her face abruptly changed from a flat and non-descript almost frown to something I could only imagine as forlorn hope. Her sparkling almond-colored eyes held a certain twinkle to them and, I imagined, she detected a twinkle or two in mine. As the song *Some Enchanted Evening* from the 1958 film *South Pacific* played in the back of my mind, *You might see a stranger across a crowded room*, it certainly was a crowded room and she, for all intents and purposes, was surely a stranger to me, but a singular question remained to be answered, in the end would it be an enchanted evening?

Chapter 22

Well, Cat was right about Cagney and Lacey. Any guy with his testosterone level functioning properly would be stepping on his drooping lips dragging across the dance floor and loosening his chastity belt if he got even a glance at them. Before I could dwell further on that thought Cagney got the ball rolling. I assumed it was Cagney anyway, judging from the sparkling silver necklace with a cursive *C* dangling from it that was doing the mambo between her more than ample and half-exposed cleavage. She sauntered right up in front of Zen, who had his arm around Miama's waist, like a slattern badly in need of a date, her marvelous dancing globes of pleasure begging for fondling.

"Get ready," Cat said, sipping her fluted glass of champagne and then it was over before it even got started.

It was like a tag-team, a good-cop-bad-cop type scenario playing itself out in real time. Lacey moved in for the kill with her own pair of fluted glasses filled with a bubbly liquid, one in each hand, as well as her pair of extraordinary dancing baubles. In an instant Zen was sandwiched between two sultry and exotic mavens of the evening, his grip on Miami's arm lost in the encounter. Soon he was sipping first from Lacey's glass and then from Cagney's, remnants of their respective red lipstick sticking not only to the fluted glasses but to Zen's lips, as well.

It was then that I made my move. I had her by the arm and was absconding with her in tow at a slow gallop through the melee of dancers, gigolos and tattooed pretenders that defined this Hawaiian love fest, Yakuza style.

In the 1950's they were known as knock-out drops. In this day and age of date rape drugs they were simply known as tablets of chloral hydrate, a colorless solid that when mixed with water produces a potent, and sometimes lethal, sedative and hypnotic effect on the unsuspecting imbiber. The unlucky imbiber in the present case was one tattooed misfit and abuser of women, Zen Takagi, and the rest, as they say, was history.

Chapter 23

"So where are we going?" Cat asked.

"A place you've never been to before," I said.

"The island of lost love?" she whimsically asked, a snippet of mischief in her sultry blue eyes.

"Close," I said. "A place close to your own heart that's begging for your appearance. Your namesake, Catalina Island."

"Oh, you mean Santa Catalina Island. It is named after a saint, you know," she said.

"Well, Missy, you are right on point, as usual," I said.

"And if you think that I am going to act anything saint-like during our little excursion, you are certainly mistaken, Mister," she said, a gleaming in her eyes that could melt steel at 50 paces and turn copper tuyeres into a molten mess.

Epilogue

Catalina Island is known for many things, including glass-bottom boats, scuba diving, and mesmerizing snorkeling escapades. It is also known for its breathtaking panoramic views of virgin sunsets hovering over the vast Pacific Ocean when late afternoons meld into gloaming violet evenings. Whether or not lost love comprises one of those many things is surely questionable. So as our two protagonists from the recent clutches of the Wasteland, Cat and James, also known as Sarge, fondly hug each other as the soft spray from the ocean drifts across their embrace, the ferry ride across the bay to Catalina Island is like an elixir that soothes the mind and the soul. For in the desultory realm known as the Wasteland, from where they have recently escaped, lost love rediscovered can surely cure many ills.

Not on Sarge's mind at the present moment is the Japanese girl on the boat. No, his mind is on the Hawaiian, at least she is half-Hawaiian, girl on the ferry. So as the approach to Santa Catalina Island nears, one question that remains in the back of Sarge's mind is whether he should change the name on his new sailboat from *Maryanne* to *Cat* or to *Catalina*. I suppose, dear reader, the outcome depends on just how saint-like our lovely D.E.A. agent on hiatus comports herself on her namesake in the next few days. One thing that is certain, however, is that

Sarge's former small sailboat will remain moored in Montrose Harbor, it being a gift newly bequeathed to Detective Fred Compton. As for Sarge's next sailboat christened with a new name, it, most assuredly, will be moored in a boat slip in the harbor of Waikiki.

As for the young and vibrant Japanese girl on the boat, otherwise known as Miama, well, matters, on occasion, do manifest themselves with favorable outcomes in the Wasteland. One would imagine that she is presently back in Chicago and safely tucked away from the sordid clutches of the Yakuza and providing oodles of information to Detective Compton and the authorities. Perhaps she will remain there in the future. Perhaps she will return to her island home. It is up to you, dear reader, to arrive at the final outcome because in the quaint and obtuse demesne known as the Wasteland nothing is for certain.

As for Detective Fred Compton, rough-around-the-edges, old school homicide detective and true purveyor of the dark underpinnings of the police subculture, one would imagine that he is presently scraping the name *Maryanne* from his newly bequeathed sailboat. What the new name will be is only conjecture. Perhaps it will be *Miami*. Perhaps he will change his mind and it will remain *Maryanne* and a new romance will birth itself. After all, she is a police psychologist and if anyone is in need of counseling, it surely is one tried-and-true and hard-as-nails homicide dick who has seen more than his fair share of malevolence that the Wasteland has to offer.

The Quondam Lover

Chapter 1

Search Warrant (12 miles Outside of Binghamton, New York)

"Cross-dresser."

"What?"

"Guy's a cross-dresser."

"Was," said Masters, nodding over her shoulder.

"Yeah, was," said Reynolds sheepishly as he emerged from the rear bedroom. "And how long we gonna' leave him hangin' up there?"

"They're still sketching the scene. Soon as the video's done," said Stone.

Stone handed the photograph to Masters. His white evidence gloves were somewhat smeared from digging deep into the cardboard box from where the photograph had originated. It was a Polaroid, black and white, from days gone by.

"Hmm, it's an old one. Haven't seen one of these in a while," said Masters, a bemused look on her face as she studied the photograph.

She was Shelly Masters, a twenty-year veteran of the F.B.I. and an expert on child abductions and juvenile sexual homicide cases. She was short, wiry and tough as nails. When God gave out looks she was at the back of the line. When God gave out brains she was at the front and that's all that mattered to Stone.

"Not exactly what we were looking for," Masters added, handing the photograph to Stone. "But it's a start."

"It's a start alright and damn quirky," said Stone.

"Huh? Just the normal creepy shit we expected to find anyway. Just bent a little bit more south than we anticipated. Black and white, that's your backyard, Stone," said Masters, with a slight smile on her face.

Stone handed her a second Polaroid.

"Now what are you thinking?" Stone asked.

"Real quirky," Masters squeaked out of her pursed lips.

Just then Trooper Bill Norton, an evidence tech on loan from the State of New York, emerged from the back bedroom carrying an old suitcase from the '60s. He set it down between Stone and Masters and flipped it open. Saying nothing, the humorous, half-assed grin of the police subculture was plastered all over his face like mud on mud-flaps and said everything.

"Yeah, damn quirky," repeated Masters after Norton had opened the suitcase.

"And there's more in the other closet," said Reynolds.

"More what?" asked Stone.

"Same shit that's in there," Norton said, pointing to the suitcase from the Vietnam era. "Bras, panties, crap like that."

"This stuff his?" asked Reynolds, pointing at the Polaroid that lay on the small table next to Stone.

Stone picked up the Polaroid and displayed it to Reynolds and Norton. It was a photograph of a man in a full Canadian Air Force uniform. The insignias on his shoulders indicated that he was a full Colonel but the head was cut-off making identification next to impossible.

"Full bird, huh?" said Reynolds. "You sure?"

Stone held up the second photograph so Reynolds and Norton could see it. It appeared to be of the same man, at least from the build, the head again being cut off, but only this time his uniform consisted of a bra and panties, and a thick rope tied succinctly around the lower portion of his neck and attached to a pulley contraption. For some odd reason, however, he was still wearing the same military jacket but open with the bra and panties fully exposed.

"Hmm, damn quirky," whispered Reynolds.

Chapter 2

12 years later (Dannemora State Prison, Upstate New York)

Miles Youngblood, a 60-year old retired major from the Canadian Air Force, sat alone at the small table as Stone entered the room.

"I knew you'd come," said Youngblood, the smirk of an arrogant sociopath adorning his banker's face.

Stone sat down across from Youngblood as the guard relocked the door and left the room.

"Why wouldn't I come?" Stone asked but then quickly added, "But before you say anything, just one more form."

"How many of those damn things do I have to sign? I'm not exactly giving you my soul, Stone."

You don't have a fucking soul, you lifeless, degenerate bastard. You're a stone-cold serial sexual sadist.

"Well, we'll see about that," smiled Stone, handing Youngblood the last form of many that had preceded his visit.

Roughly scribbling his signature on the form, Youngblood's cuffed hands nudged it forward toward Stone, who slowly tucked it away among the other forms previously signed by the sociopath.

"Pen, please," said Stone.

"Oh, you've been watching *Silence of the Lambs*, have you? You believe in all of that mumbo-jumbo and abracadabra shit, Stone?"

Stone took the pen from dead fingers and placed it safely in his shirt pocket.

"You don't like me, do you?" smugly asked Youngblood.

"Does it really matter? In the long-run, I mean?"

"Depends on what you mean by the long-run. Wouldn't happen to have a cigarette, would you, Stone?" Youngblood asked, his fingers tapping out the tune of nicotine withdrawal on the gray metal table born of interrogation rooms and holding cells.

"Let's see if we get anywhere first. I hate to waste cigarettes on sociopaths who tell me nothing of value."

Youngblood coughed out a stale laugh.

"I like your style, Stone. I knew you'd be different from the others. Talking over the phone can be so terse at times but deep down here I felt some vibes," said Youngblood, indicating his midsection where some believed a person's soul dwelled. "And I actually looked forward to your calls. You too?"

"I think they were your calls."

"Our conversations, let's put it that way. That's common ground, isn't it? Learn anything from our conversations, Stone? From a psychological point of view, I mean?"

"What other point of view is there?"

"*Touché*! Now we're getting somewhere. So how about that cigarette, Stone, since you've got my engine revved up and idling at high speed?"

Stone removed a pack of death from his pants pocket and slid it across the table to the sociopath. Cold and calculating fingers removed a filtered cigarette and then twirled it in the damp and fetid prison air as if it were a wand.

"Gotta' light it up for me, sport," smiled Youngblood.

"Sport? You're aging yourself. Isn't that something Clark Gable would have said to Loretta Young?"

"Before or after he knocked her up?"

Gray, tarry smoke and noisome breath smelling of dank prison cells and rusted iron bars encircled the sociopath's face seconds after Stone lit the cigarette.

"Ah, much better. Now, where were we?"

"You were about to confess to me," said Stone.

Youngblood's eyes floated in a sea of contrived deceit. A gallows smirk appeared on his tired and worn-out face, as if he were waiting for the moutons to fall and the blade of the guillotine to drop.

"Ah, well, Stone, you're not like all of those other so-called psychologists and mind readers who sat across from me with their legs crossed and their hands religiously folded, as if they were in the front pew at midnight mass, and then asking me all those pointless and silly questions, spewing out Labeling Theory and Restorative Justice, whatever the hell that crap is anyway, ultimately trying to arrive at some final answer to the question of what makes old Mister Youngblood tick. I hate all those sorry pricks and their phony theories. That's all that shit is anyway, Stone, theories and statistics, you know that from your Academy days. Yeah, let's get right to the fucking point here, Stone. I've got something of value and you want it."

"And what's that?" asked Stone.

"A unique insight into the real meaning of evil, up-front and personal evil, the kind to which you have never been exposed, Stone. The shit that'll make the hairs on the back of your neck point to the sun and then dance an Irish jig. That's why you're here, isn't it?"

"You don't appreciate the wrongfulness of your acts. That's what I want to understand. That's what's wrong with you.

Socially responsible, hell, you're socially irresponsible. That's why I came here and for your confession, of course."

"My confession? Don't priests hear one's confession, Stone? Oh, I suppose then that F.B.I. Agents have a lot in common with men of the cloth, eh, Stone," he said, an unholy sneer plastered across his unrepentant face.

Stone said nothing, refusing to give the repulsive sociopath an opening.

"That's the psychoanalytic bullshit that you've been force-fed and brainwashed with your entire adult life. The simple fact is, Agent Stone, I just think differently than you do."

"So you do understand that your criminal acts are wrong then?"

"Of course, Stone. I may be a degenerate from your point of view but I'm certainly not an idiot. My thinking, my logic, is that of a sociopath, not a psychopath, for your edification. I've offended society. The mere psychopath is no more than a pathological liar and narcissist and, more often than not, just a common adulterer and philanderer who hasn't taken that next wonderful step into the world of criminality. We sociopaths, Stone, well, our brains are just wired uniquely. Our neurons fire differently than yours. It's not your logic or your passion. You know what a sociopath is, don't you, Stone?"

"Sure. I'm talking to one, aren't I?"

"Exactly. Talking to but not talking with. You note the difference, don't you, as subtle as it is?"

"I didn't know a sociopath could be subtle?"

"Why not? We're pathological liars, aren't we? Manipulators? Narcissists? We dwell in the abyss of self-aggrandizement and lack of remorse that's uncommon to you church-going bastards. Save your holy water and your Our Fathers for another day, Stone. But don't you see it? There's an innate subtleness there, Stone, don't you agree? When you really look deeply into it, the Abyss, I mean, don't you feel it? You have looked into the Abyss, haven't you, Stone?"

"Never have been there," said Stone. "The Abyss, that's your provenance."

"Oh, but you do want to get there, don't you? Just to see what it's like. Deep down in the bowels of it and squirming around with all of the other non-believers, hmm? How about a kitchen pass to the Abyss, Stone? You'd like that, wouldn't you? Fear of the dark, fear of heights, fear of thunder and lightning, fear of spiders and of women, and surrounded by all of the other latent fears that persist into adolescence, well, they persist forever in the Abyss, Stone. All those fears, quondam foes to most, but quondam lovers to us sociopaths, yes, Stone, you've tried to get there. You've tried to think like us, haven't you? But the simple fact is you've miserably failed."

"Think like you? Oh, you mean like a degenerate, self-absorbed miscreant with a hollow soul, that is, if you have ever even possessed a soul. Doesn't every investigative psychologist view you in that regard?"

"Oh, so that's what you're calling yourself these days. Has a nice ring to it, hmm, doesn't it? *In-ves-ti-ga-tive* psychologist but what happened to criminal profiler and all of that other smarmy CSI crap? Stop watching TV, Stone?"

"Does it really matter?"

"Must have. You've changed your moniker, haven't you?"

The sociopath breathed in deeply, appearing to luxuriate in his false bravado.

"But you're right. It really doesn't matter, Stone. Because you'll never get in here as much as you try," he said, tapping his head with his bony and deformed index finger. "Just as you live in a world of specialized work, we sociopaths live in a world of our own unique and demoralized perceptions."

Stone's eyes fixated on the gray deadness of the sociopath's face and the stale disregard for humanity in his eyes.

"No, Stone. The Abyss is off-limits to you. It's a curious place for you novices to think about and plan day-trips into but you'll only get as far as this."

Youngblood slowly swept his pale hand across his face and the static, desolate look of the sociopath metamorphosed into the smiling, alluring face of the cost accountant that he had once been in civilian life after his retirement from the air force.

"So that's how it works? It's that simple?"

"Yeah, as simple as two plus two equals five."

Youngblood's hand swept across his face again but slowly from top to bottom and then the face of the sociopath reemerged in full malevolence. It was the death shroud of absolute evil that was difficult to define but which Stone recognized immediately.

"You'll never understand how it works, Stone."

Stone stared into lifeless eyes.

"Try as you might, Stone, you'll never really get it," he callously smirked.

Youngblood's lips were thin-lined and claylike in appearance. His eyes then began to twinkle in vindictive delight, changing like a chameleon displays its various colors, as he appeared to play with Stone's mind. Stone breathed shallowly, sucking in the dregs of clues that emanated from the sociopath's machinations, like the remnants of DNA fragments lingering at crime scenes or like stale blood oozing from a sutured wound.

"But that's why you're really here, isn't it, Stone? To get it. Maybe for your next book, hmmm, or for the next class that you'll teach at the Academy? Well, sorry about that. I mean, maybe you should retake Psych 101."

"You mean rehabilitation is a myth?"

The sociopath vehemently laughed, coughing up chaos and disorder.

"You know there's no such thing. Rehabilitation and remorse, hah, I am what I am. I am where I was. There's no way out of the Abyss, Stone, once you're in it. Of all people, you should know that first hand."

"Then what about understanding?"

The sociopath's face turned blank, an unwritten page waiting to be blotted with the murky ink of deceit and manipulation.

"Sure, I suppose that's possible. First, do this. Go out and find a nice, little, smiling nine-year-old girl, bludgeon her over the back of her head with a metal rod, stuff her into the trunk of your car, drive to a secluded area and then pull out all of her fingernails with a pair of pliers, that is, after you have had your way with her. That should get you a free pass into the Abyss, Stone. Maybe, but then do stop by again and we'll have a nice little chat about it, a little one-on-one, a *tete-a-tete* shall we say, one sociopath to the other, hmm, just to make sure."

Stone felt like sucker-punching Youngblood between his deadened and lifeless eyes but that's what Youngblood wanted, getting a rise out of Stone, gaining the upper-hand, securing an advantage. So Stone quickly moved on.

"And?"

"Stone, we just think differently than you do-gooders. We're talking life patterns here, ways of surviving within ourselves. That will take a lifetime for you to understand."

"I have time."

Youngblood tapped his head.

"No, Stone. There's not enough time to get in here."

Youngblood slowly leaned back into his prison chair that was as stiff as his muted stare and then hollow silence undulated cautiously between crime-fighter and career criminal like the vibrating strings of an old and tired violin.

"Then why did you call me and request this meeting in the first place?" asked Stone.

"Because I need something. Why else would a sociopath reach out to a, well, to an esteemed investigative psychologist?"

"What exactly is it that you need?"

Chapter 3

The Knowles Nursing Home, Syracuse, New York

"Letter for you, Doctor," said the intern, handing the smudged missive to Doctor Samuel Barnes.

"Thank you, Roy," said Barnes, his trembling hands clutching the letter as he settled himself back in his recliner, the rancid excuse for a blanket pulled up tightly around his neck.

The stale scent of fear wafted upwards from his urine-soaked pajamas, as if a dreaded premonition was about to be proclaimed. The envelope was marked legal and private. The return address was that of Inmate #2423, Miles Youngblood, Dannemora State Prison. Barnes opened the letter nervously, remembering that nothing good could come from an encounter with Youngblood.

My good Doctor,

Please indulge your favorite patient (remember once a patient, always a patient) with a small favor. You will soon have a visitor, a Mr.

*Stone, inquiring for the key that I left with
you. Please give it to him. And do remember
our last session before I was arrested; oh, so long
ago. About twelve years, wasn't it? Right after
that boyfriend of yours hung himself wearing
my old air force uniform, hmm? Never should
have let you have it in the first place. Oh, well,
that really doesn't matter now but time does fly
when one is, well, having as much fun as I am.
Thanks much for the memories.*

Your favorite patient

Barnes could not control his bowels and soon he was
soaking wet. He dropped the letter to the floor and slumped
back miserably in his chair. He pushed off the ragged blanket
into the warm puddle of fresh urine that had formed beside
his bed and attempted to wipe up the mess with his foot. The
letter was now floating in the rancid pool, soaking up warm
urine. He called for the intern and soon Roy appeared.

"Please, I'm sorry. I …"

"No problem, Doc. I'm used to it," said Roy, looking down
at the floor. "But what about the letter. Should I …"

"No, no, no. Just … I don't need it. Just …"

"Sure, I'll get rid of it with the blanket and we'll get you
all changed up nice and neat like, okay?"

As Roy scooped up the urine-soaked blanket he turned to
Barnes and said, "Hope it was a good letter."

Barnes lost control again as soon as Roy left the room.

Chapter 4

The Knowles Nursing Home,
Syracuse, New York

"He died in his sleep last night, Agent Stone. Heart attack followed by a stroke, it must have been relatively painless but the expression on his face when the orderly found him was, well, quite contorted."

Stone listened attentively as Dr. Morris Williams, the physician in charge, recounted the facts surrounding the sudden death of another one of his contemporaries, Dr. Samuel Barnes, a retired psychiatrist from Syracuse.

"I suppose this is for you. It has your name on it," said Dr. Williams, pushing a small envelope toward Stone from across his desk. "He was clutching it in one of his hands when we found him. Looks like he was expecting you. He earlier had left a scribbled message with the orderly that someone would be stopping by to see him and to give the envelope to that person. It looks like you are that person."

"Thanks much, Doctor, and, by the way if I may ask, for what was he being treated?"

"Well, you being an F.B.I. Agent, well, I suppose it is all right to discuss that, seeing that he is, well, off to a better place now. You know he was a psychiatrist before he became a patient here."

"Yes, that I did know," said Stone.

"Well, it seems that he had his own set of peculiarities. Maybe the dregs of evil that he dealt with on a regular basis somehow rubbed off on him over the years. Anyway, in his later years he became obsessed with autoerotic fantasies and damned near killed himself, almost broke his neck on one occasion."

"Hanging?"

"Yes, quite a contraption he had rigged up in his office, ropes, pulleys and intricate release knots, you get the picture. Anyway, that's what wound up bringing him here. His family had simply had about enough of his peculiar antics. Anyway, we're really not a nursing home, Agent Stone, even though that's the name that is on our door."

"Yes?"

"We're kind of an in-between, a medical Limbo, if you will, the last step before a full-blown commitment, shall we say," said Dr. Williams.

"Involuntary commitment?'

"Exactly, it seems that he got mixed up with underage youth when he was practicing his so-called art of voluntary asphyxiation. So after his family had requested, really begged is a more accurate description, the authorities to place him here and avoid the embarrassment and ridicule involuntary commitment as a sex offender would offer, well, here is where he was placed."

"But he wasn't convicted of any sex crimes, at least that's what the records show."

"Right, avoided it completely, well, not exactly completely," said Dr. Williams. "He entered into an agreement with the State, not a formal plea agreement exactly, and that so-called agreement is what placed him here, ostensibly to seek rehabilitation. The document is sealed, the agreement that is, and so no one will ever know but now you know, Agent Stone."

"I see."

"But this is all confidential, Agent Stone, as you earlier informed me when you called. Just for lead purposes, I think those were your exact words."

"Yes, confidentiality, you have my word on it," said Stone rising, the small yellowed envelope clutched in his hand.

"And what's in that envelope, Agent Stone? Any idea?"

Stone carefully placed the envelope in his jacket pocket, as if it contained a sacred relic, and then looked squarely into the eyes of Dr. Williams.

"I imagine that it is going to unlock a Pandora's box of evil," Stone said, a severe and wrinkled crease stretching across his forehead.

Chapter 5

Dannemora State Prison, Upstate New York

"Well, I see that you were a little too late, Stone," said Youngblood. "It was in all of the newspapers. I read about it. Too bad, heart attacks can be so sudden, don't you think?"

"He knew I was coming. He had the envelope in his hands when he died."

"Exacerbated his death, is that what you are thinking?" asked Youngblood, his toes in his prison-issued, blue and laceless sneakers tapping out a beat to *Yankee Doodle Dandy* on the cold and unforgiving cracked cement floor.

"I'm sure you wanted it that way," said Stone. "One less witness with which to deal."

"Hah, you are so right! Now how about what's in the envelope, hmm, Stone?"

Stone emptied the lone contents of the tarnished and yellowed envelope onto the dull gray interview table. It clinked with the sound of a jailer's keys being brandished in front of a disgruntled inmate's face as it landed on the metallic surface. Youngblood frantically reached for it but was held fast by his restraints. Being shackled to the table, his grasp was a click short of reaching the key.

"You bastard, Stone, having fun, are you?" seethed Youngblood, the jagged veins in his granular face that resembled old parchment papers from the Smithsonian throbbing spastically.

"Must be very important to you," said Stone, leaning back in his chair and regarding the sociopathic killer with contempt.

"*Quid pro quo*, is that it, Stone? I told you that I would introduce you to evil. I kept my part of the bargain. Now you know and you should fully realize that Barnes, that so-called psychiatrist, that degenerate and autoerotic freak, was into some real kinky shit. Do a little more digging and you might find the dead bodies of those missing runaways he had enticed into his autoerotic lair, hmm? Now the key, Stone, pass it over," grunted Youngblood in his monotonic and stale prison voice.

"How many bodies?" asked Stone, treading on insecure ground, guessing really, but just trying to keep up the charade of knowing more than he really did.

"C'mon, Stone," said Youngblood, his facial expression normalizing into that of the cost accountant he had once been. "Twelve years ago, that search warrant in Binghamton, remember? Botched it up really good, didn't you, you and your cronies? Anonymous tip, wasn't it? Got a search warrant that didn't hold up in court. Lost everything. Everybody walked but you did stumble onto some photos, right? And the deadbeat hanging from the rafters in that pathetic farmhouse and wearing one of my old military uniforms, eh, quite curious, wasn't it? Didn't know that then but now you do. Just a drifter, a nobody Barnes found wandering around the train tracks when he was searching for runaways and using a bunch of misfits and hoboes to help him, just the last piece to the puzzle good old Barnes needed for his autoerotic electric show."

Stone's thought process was traveling a mile a minute. He flashed back to that rundown farmhouse on the outskirts of Binghamton twelve years ago and the anonymous tip that had led him there searching for runaway boys who he feared had been murdered and now it appeared that that mysterious anonymous tipster from what seemed like light years ago was arrogantly seated across from him and secured with heavy prison shackles. Staring him square in the eyes he read *Gotcha,' Stone* in the cesspool of Youngblood's bloated irises. Youngblood, however, was right. He'd been too hasty. The search warrant just wasn't sound but he had proceeded anyway, smelling victory, which eventually had turned into defeat.

"That was Barnes' deal, plain and simple. Right, good old Barnes, master of contraptions, plastic bags over the head, and intricately tied slip-knots and you found the one unfortunate slug who couldn't release the damn slip-knot and hung himself, and now you have the photos, Stone. I'm sure that they are safely tucked away in some rotting and mildewed file cabinet in a damp basement somewhere with all of your other unsolved cold cases and just waiting to be resurrected. Dead files, Stone, just gathering dust, eh? Accidental death, isn't that what you concluded, hmm, Stone? But you never did find the bodies of any runaways, did you? That little secret is neatly tucked away forever in the putrefying mind of Barnes. He's dead now and not coming back, if you haven't noticed, Stone," said Youngblood, a lined smile on his dull and lifeless face.

Youngblood's eyes were riveted on the key that Stone now held in his hand, which Stone was tossing up in the air and then catching, as if it were an apple for the teacher.

"But you screwed up," said Stone. "You wanted Barnes out of the way because he knew too much. So you called in the marker. You were the anonymous tipster but you didn't know that all of your cross-dressing paraphernalia, your frilly girlie underwear and bras, would still be there. Seems that Barnes had a thing for it, for you too, probably, hmm? Afternoon kissing cousins, something like that, wasn't it?" asked Stone, attempting to get a rise out of the sociopath.

The sociopath's deadened stare remained inflexible, the cold and gray prison walls of the interrogation room his accomplices, the stale air of incarceration his co-conspirator.

"That was your air force uniform but, lucky for you, the face in the Polaroids had been cut off and that suitcase full of all those tarnished trinkets and girlie stuff, that was yours, too, wasn't it?"

"Doing your homework, I see, Stone, but just a tad too late. It doesn't pay to be tardy in your business, does it? Oh, well, that's nice and dandy but you'll never prove any of that nonsense and, besides, you came up empty anyway. Barnes is dead, no bodies were recovered, and a photo without a face, well, that's about as good as a slip-knot that doesn't slip, eh, Stone," laughed the sociopath.

"But I have something you want," said Stone, fingering the key as if he were going to unlock something.

"And I have something you want, Stone," Youngblood said, gently tapping his forehead. "But it's locked up in here nice and tight and you can't get in because you don't have the key. So we are at an unfortunate impasse, it seems. Now let's make a deal, shall we?"

"A deal? You're a pathetic crossdresser whose gender identity is misconstrued, someone who lured little boys into engaging in perverted fantasies with your pathetic friend and sometime lover, Barnes, hmm, am I right?"

"You are being pedantic, Stone, calling me vulgar names. That will get you nowhere. Now move to the back of the classroom, will you, and take a seat where you belong and I will give you lesson number one in understanding evil. Simply give the key to the attendant who is patiently waiting outside of the door. He will place it with my other belongings and then I'll tell you where the bodies are buried. You see, I had nothing to do with it, really, just a mere spectator, so to speak, and with Barnes dead you'll never prove a damn thing against me anyway. Barnes is your man but, oh, I forgot, he's as dead as Marley's ghost. Now ante up, Stone, or pack up your trinkets and get the fuck out of here and quit wasting my time."

The small interrogation room with its tired walls of peeling gray paint and with no windows was closing in on Stone. The key he held in his hand felt like a white-hot branding iron eating into his flesh and as the cool and subdued eyes of the malignant sociopath regarded him, it was as if he was an unequal player in this game of good versus evil on the edge of the Abyss between Heaven and Hell. He dejectedly felt as if there was no way out.

"So what will it be, eh, Stone?" Youngblood asked, the face of a satisfied miscreant holding center stage. "Your key for mine, hmm?"

Chapter 6

Stone placed the key onto the table in front of him. It was a small copper-colored key and seemed appropriate for someone with small hands. There was no inscription whatsoever on it, just a small and tarnished metal key that looked as if it might fit into an intricate mechanism and surely too small to fit into a lockbox.

He then dialed up Shelly Masters' phone number. Stone hadn't really talked with her in quite some time, as she had been transferred back to FBIHQ and was now working in the Crimes Against Children Section. He waited patiently as the hollow ringing reverberated in his ears, hoping that she would be of some help. Finally, she answered. Her voice had not changed one iota since they had last conversed almost two years ago. So after the perfunctory reminiscences were played out Stone got right to the point.

"I need you to pull a closed file for me. Remember that case from Binghamton almost twelve years ago? It should fit in with exactly what you are doing back at headquarters," said Stone.

"Got something good, do you?" Masters responded.

"Could be. I've been dealing with a potential subject on another matter and he tipped the scales in that direction."

"Where?" she asked.

"Upstate New York, he's incarcerated at Dannemora."

"That piss-hole?"

"Exactly."

"Still assigned to Albany, I see," said Masters. "You must like the trees and the snow up there."

"It puts my mind at ease, the serenity, but you wouldn't understand that, being back in the bowels of the beast in Washington."

"Real funny, Stone. So what do you need exactly?" asked Masters.

"The dead guy hanging from the rafters in that old farm house, well, he's really of no significance, just a drifter who was in the wrong place at the wrong time."

"But what about the air force uniform the guy was wearing, not his and just a prop?"

"Right, the uniform belonged to a guy named Miles Youngblood. He's doing life without parole in Dannemora. They got him for a double homicide with real aggravating circumstances."

"Like?" she asked.

"Both victims were prostitutes, decapitated and dismembered. He eviscerated both of them with a scuba knife."

"Monster of Florence stuff?" asked Masters.

"It appears that there are some commonalities present. Maybe he's just an enthusiast in this kind of stuff and reads a lot but evidence of necrophilia was introduced at trial, as well, and that seemed to have swayed the judge. He'll never see the light of day."

"And how did you hook up with this cretin? Checking out Craig's List, were you?"

Stone suppressed a laugh.

"He contacted me out of the blue and said he'd give me a real life view of evil. Up front and personal were his exact words."

"Oh, he's been reading your articles, has he? The last one on Intimate Partner Violence was very informative. So you got the go-ahead to talk with him?"

"Right."

"But you weren't expecting this?"

"Not in a million years. It was just a shot in the dark, a needle in a haystack, so to speak, you know, one less sociopath to interview in my illustrious career."

"You're being too modest, Stone. Aren't you scheduled to lecture at the F.B.I. Academy one of these days?" she asked.

"Next week and I was hoping to meet up with you in Quantico then and discuss this case. Do you think you would have time to pull the file and review it by then?"

"Anything for you, Stone. You know that."

"I knew I could count on you."

"Just one other thing," she said.

"Yes?"

"What does he want? They always want something."

Stone fingered the small key, hoping that something would rub off on him. Perhaps a clue or possibly the innate dregs of evil that he inferred that it portended would manifest themselves.

"He wants what I have. It's a small key. He wants it really badly and he appears ready to give up the location of the bodies of those kids we were looking for twelve years ago to get his hands on it."

"And into what does the key fit?"

"Damned if I know. I am hoping that you might find something in the file that would shed some light on that curious question."

"Needle in a haystack, Stone," she said. "Shot in the dark?"

"Exactly."

Chapter 7

F.B.I. Academy (Quantico, Virginia)

"So how did the lecture go?" asked Masters.

"The usual," said Stone. "Psychosexual asphyxiation is always a big hit, you know that from your Academy days."

"Long time ago, Stone," she said.

They were seated in a small room near the library, Masters with her assorted photocopies from the cold case file that Stone had requested her to review spread out in front of her, as if she was reading the comics on Sunday morning. Stone, with a grimace on his face that was his typical way of hoping for a breakthrough, waited patiently as she organized her work.

"Show me the key," said Masters.

Stone removed the small envelope from his jacket pocket and deftly removed the small, tarnished metal key and placed it on the table between them.

"You're right. It is quite small," she said. "Certainly not a lockbox key."

"Any ideas come to mind?" asked Stone. "He really wants it. Damned near broke his wrist trying to reach for it when I showed it to him. Handcuffs can be so annoying at times."

Masters smiled and then picked up the key, placing it in the palm of her hand. Her face was drawn taut, as if she were measuring her thoughts in a graduated cylinder that was about to be emptied into an empty flask.

"There is something," she said, as she reached into her briefcase and retrieved a small watch.

Stone listened intently.

"I found this buried under the box of photographs that we found at the scene. Never gave it a second thought," she said. "Just a wristwatch, it appears, possibly a lady's watch and maybe just more of that girlie shit they were wearing but when you turn it over, well, take a look."

Stone picked up the wristwatch and then turned it over, setting it on the table.

"See the two openings equidistant apart. It looks like a key might fit into them."

"Two keys or the same key?" asked Stone.

"Tread lightly. Remember, this is a devious son-of-a-bitch we're dealing with. Could be booby-trapped in some odd way."

Stone placed the key into the small opening on the left but did not turn it. It fit snugly. He removed it and then attempted to place it into the opening on the right but it didn't fit.

"Different keys," said Stone.

"Now what?" asked Masters.

"Well, there must be a second key but, surely, there's something in there that he desperately wants and if we turn the key the wrong way it could destroy it. It appears that we need that second key."

"Okay."

"Possibly the other key needs to be placed into the other opening and both keys turned at once, otherwise we could lose for whatever we are looking," said Stone.

"Why don't we just give it to the Toolmarks Section down the hall and let them have a go at it?" she asked.

"Or get the other key."

"Are you thinking what I'm thinking?" she asked.

"Yeah, he's got it somewhere."

"But where?"

"Good question."

Chapter 8

F.B.I. Laboratory (Toolmarks Section)

"Fuming nitric acid, see the discoloration it makes," said the toolmark technician, pointing to a brownish-yellow piece of cloth. "Get that stuff on your hands and your flesh turns into runny, black molasses and you'll need a gallon or two of paint remover just to get the dark stains to disappear."

His name was Brent Townsend and he had the resolve of a gladiator in the arena when plying his trade. His specialty was interpreting toolmarks, how they were made, and what instrumentality made them, and now he was focused on a rather common looking woman's wristwatch that was laid face down on his investigative work bench, as he toyed with the small metal key that Stone had given to him.

"Take a look at the x-ray, Stone," he said, pointing to a small darkened area on the x-ray.

"Yes," said Stone.

"Okay, you were right about the key. It fits only one of the openings on the watch and judging from the small blips that you can see next to the darkened area in the x-ray, it appears that both keys have to be turned at the same time and in opposite directions or ..."

"Or?" asked Stone.

"It's built to self-destruct. It's a failsafe mechanism, Stone. Whatever devious prick constructed this, it appears that if someone were to turn the keys the wrong way, or simply force them into an opening into which they didn't fit, well, then all hell would break loose and fuming nitric acid would be released that would dissolve whatever it was that one was looking for inside of the watch."

"How do you know it's nitric acid?"

"Well, we can tell that there is a small ampule like receptacle, here," he said, pointing to the x-ray. "And that it's most probably made of glass. So it can't be hydrofluoric acid that it contains because that acid is used to etch glass and just wouldn't be stable over time. So it's got to contain a different mineral acid, a strong acid that would destroy anything with which it came into contact. Hydrochloric acid would work and so would sulfuric acid but if one really wanted to make a sheer mess of things, I'd wager the bastard decided to use fuming nitric acid. Just a guess, Stone, but I think that's our best bet at this juncture."

"So if one were to force the lock mechanism, the glass ampule would be broken and acid would be released which would eat away the insides of the watch?"

"Right, almost immediately but what do you think it contains that's so important to construct such an intricate device? It's almost like building a ship in a bottle."

"What about a microchip or something like that?" asked Stone.

"Nah, it would have shown up on the x-ray. We took a bunch of shots and from numerous angles and nothing like that was indicated."

"What about microfilm, like in the old days?"

"What? Wear a tie, catch a spy? Cold War, Stone? Berlin Wall stuff?" asked Townsend. "You're dating yourself, Stone."

"Maybe it's a just game to him. Cat and mouse, spy versus spy? The guy just doesn't think like us. His brain is wired with reverse engineering and soldered with hatred and contempt for human decency."

"Okay, so what would the microfilm contain?" asked Townsend.

"Well, what does microfilm usually contain?" asked Stone.

"Numbers? Integers? Dots and dashes? Maybe Morse Code stuff? I'm thinking Enigma machine material, Stone? What's your guess? What does he have that you need from him that maybe he doesn't really have but is just blowing smoke up your ass?"

"Bluffing?" asked Stone.

"Could be. He's a demented low-life, isn't he, Stone? Pathological liar and absorbed in his own little fantasy world of mystery and mayhem, hmm? What does he have that you need?"

It was like a laser beam aimed at Stone's midbrain. It was as if his neurons had anticipated the question. Suddenly, Stone remembered an old saying that his mother used all the time – *The egg must be broken before the omelet can be made.* What had Youngblood promised? The location of the dead runaways but did he really know? Or was he just bluffing in that irrational way that sociopaths have monopolized time and time again over the millennium? So now it appeared that the egg was the wristwatch that lay on the table in front of him and the omelet was the undisclosed location of dead victims.

"It could be a location," blurted out Stone.

"A location, hmm, but a disguised location and maybe only something he would recognize and could decode but not us."

Stone waited.

"Numbers are easy to place on microfilm, Stone. Integers, zeroes and ones, just like in a computer. Even dots and dashes, perhaps. Numbers, locations? Maybe latitude and longitude, who would know what the hell it all meant?" said Townsend.

"Only someone who was looking for dead bodies, somebody like Youngblood. Somebody who could sway the system and use the location of dead bodies as leverage."

"Leverage? For what?"

"Sentence reduction, remember, he's doing what amounts to a life sentence," said Stone.

"Based upon what you just told me, they'll never let that bastard out," said Townsend.

"How many dead bodies are we looking at?" asked Stone.

"Damned if I know," said Townsend.

"Exactly."

"Right," said Townsend.

"Now how do we open it without releasing the acid?" asked Stone getting anxious.

"Very carefully," said Townsend. "I made another key and it fits nicely into the other opening."

Townsend handed the key to Stone, smiling.

"Ready to give it a go, partner? Worst thing that can happen is that you might get an ugly acid burn on your fingernails, maybe even lose a finger or two," said Townsend, an unholy smirk plastered across his face compliments of the police subculture.

Chapter 9

Dannemora State Prison

"Found the watch, did you? Well, that was the plan anyway," said the sociopath, apparently eyeing the blackened fingernails on Stone's right hand. "Fuming nitric acid can be so annoying at times, don't you think?"

"Only a devious bastard like you would think of using it," said Stone, placing the discolored wristwatch face down on the interview table between them.

Youngblood casually smiled, a smile born of remorseless miscreants that inhabit the Abyss.

"So do you have the microfilm or did you gum it all up with acid, hmm?"

"Right here," said Stone, patting his jacket pocket.

"Okay, so have you figured it out yet or have you lost your Boy Scout handbook? Dots and dashes, Stone? Morse Code, remember? I'm sure you were an Eagle Scout in your misspent youth. You have that pedantic look about you and that annoying temperament it takes to be one. Order of the Arrow too, probably, hmm?"

Stone had been an Eagle Scout and the sociopath was right on the other count, as well. Maybe he had just done his homework and researched his bio or maybe he was just a calculating son-of-bitch that read people as well as Stone did.

"You too, I suppose, but probably never made Tenderfoot, though, I would guess."

"Second Class, hah," laughed Youngblood, his gray-black tongue lingering on his thin and brittle lips. "You are dead-on, Stone. Just couldn't get that *good-deed-for-a-day* thing right. It just wasn't in me, genetic probably, you know, nature and nurture stuff. I'm sure you understand."

The sociopath's darkened eyes were riveted on Stone's face, as if he were sizing up a target.

"Now why don't you just let me take a gander at that microfilm that's so comfortably secreted in your jacket pocket, hmmm, and we'll both have a go at deciphering it, shall we?" he asked, intentionally lisping at the end of his words like a nervous librarian would who didn't know how to use the Dewey Decimal System.

"What's the rush, sport, you got a hot date? Oops, I forgot you're doing life without parole. Sorry about that, chum."

Youngblood eased back into his pre-intimidation position. His legs were shackled to the interview table and his hands were handcuffed in the front of his body. He lifted up his hands to scratch his face, which displayed the remnants of a day or two's growth of spotted and red-gray facial hair.

"So that's the way you want to play it. Oh, well, have it your way," he laconically said and then began whistling *Dixie* under his fetid breath, which smelled of abject rancor.

"What exactly is it that you want, Youngblood?" asked Stone. "Time to stop playing games."

"You know what happened in 2007, don't you?" asked the sociopath.

"Yeah, the Red Sox won the World Series."

"Hah, how curt you are, Stone. I just love it when you play hardball. Right, so anyway for your edification the death penalty in New York was declared unconstitutional."

Stone only smiled knowing somewhat where Youngblood was headed with his demented logic.

"And I was the last lucky prick on death row to be reprieved, so to speak," said Youngblood.

"Too bad. If they had kept it, I would have attended your going away party; wouldn't have missed it for the world and, by the way, you would have loved it, too. Sodium thiopental can be so relaxing, don't you think?" asked Stone.

Youngblood leaned as close as he could to Stone's face.

"There's rumblings about that they are going to bring it back. Some upstarts from Albany are behind it."

"And?" asked Stone.

"Well, it's not too complicated, Stone. I want the hell out of here. Someplace nice and breezy with warm air wafting past my window. I want out of New York's penal system, plain and simple. That's what I want, a fucking window with a view, Stone. The federal joint in Lompoc would do just fine with all that lazy California ocean air pumping across the bay and they have tennis courts there, too."

The sociopath then gave his best impression of what swinging a tennis racket in handcuffs would look like and then smiled, his deadened and rust-colored teeth somewhat biting his lower lip, as if he had just scored an ace at Wimbledon.

"Right," said Stone. "But it looks like you could use a lesson or two and, by the way, you are here on a state charge if my memory serves me correctly. Lompoc is a Federal prison. Let's not mix apples and oranges, shall we?"

"You can swing it, sport. Just get the wardens to sign off with a simple-minded prosecutor thrown into the mix or some half-ass state senator who needs the publicity and a donation to his campaign fund. You can do it, Stone. Finding dead bodies, kids' bodies especially, is sure to make the front pages of any half-decent rag and then jump-start some political overachiever's career, don't you think? Pump up his or her cesspool of donated funds, hmm?"

"And if I set it up, then what?"

"Then I'll decipher all of those little silly ass dots and dashes on the microfilm that's comfortably secreted in your breast pocket and I'll tell you where that devious amateur, Barnes, hid the bodies. You know, there are twelve of them in all," sardonically stated the sociopath, grinning and leaning back in his prison-issued jumpsuit, an ugly, dark, inky blue color, the kind of deflated blue, Stone imagined, with which the sociopath's lost soul was painted.

Chapter 10

The Office of the Warden – Dannemora State Prison

"He wants what?" asked the Warden.

He was Warden Thomas Hawkins and he had been the Warden at Dannemora for only a short period of time, having spent the bulk of his 30-year career on the west coast, mostly in jails and holding facilities in Fresno and Modesto, and with a long stint as a guard at San Quentin.

"It's all there in his request," said Stone, pushing the document across Hawkins' desk. "It appears that he has unique and valuable information."

"They all have information, Mr. Stone. It's their only ploy to get the hell out of here," Hawkins said, a stale look to his prison-hardened eyes.

"Twelve bodies, at least that's what he says," said Stone.

"An even dozen, hmm," said Hawkins. "And you believe him?"

"As much as anyone can believe a sociopath."

"This request is right out of a dime novel, Stone," said the man seated next to Hawkins. "Been reading too many Nancy Drew stories, have you?"

He was the Principal Legal Adviser for the prison and he supervised all matters dealing with prisoner complaints, *habeas corpus* proceedings, and Section 1983 cases involving the deprivation of constitutional rights. He was stiff, non-compliant and unfriendly. In short, he exhibited the exact attributes that prison lawyers envied.

"Anything is possible when one considers the end results. If he is telling the truth and he does know where the bodies are, then who gives a good Goddamn if he spends the rest of his putrid existence in a state prison or a federal facility? Frankly, I don't and I suggest that you get the Governor on board with this and have him sign the damn papers," said Stone, his tone somewhat exasperated.

"How do you know he has the information and is not just bluffing like they all do?" asked the lawyer, pen in hand and nervously tapping it on the scarred metal desk, as if he was uncomfortable not writing out some kind of writ or slashing a big fat red *X* across a prisoner's grievance.

"I know one thing," said Stone. "I know there is an opportunity here."

"There was an opportunity at Gettysburg on the third day and that just didn't work out very well for Pickett," said the lawyer, his face reeking of *res ipsa loquitor*.

Stone eased back in his chair and thought for a moment. He had given a copy of the coded message he had removed from the wristwatch to the Document Section at FBIHQ and had been waiting feverishly for a phone call but now this impasse had presented itself. It wasn't exactly Pickett's Charge that confronted him, but it was pretty damn close. Maybe he should just fold up shop and give the damn microfilm to Youngblood and see what the sociopath could come up with but would he tell Stone the truth without a deal, without getting that free pass to Lompoc?

"It's an opportunity, nonetheless," said Stone, drilling holes into the sarcastic-looking eyes of the prison lawyer. "And if successful, it could really jump-start, so to speak, one's career, if one, of course, had a career worth jump-starting and were predisposed to that sort of thing."

Stone noted a slight glimmering in the prison lawyer's eyes, as if he had just scored a bulls-eye.

Chapter 11

Dannemora State Prison

Stone slid the microfilm across the table to Youngblood.

"Didn't gum it up too badly, did you?" asked Youngblood, his bloated eyes appearing to begin to digest the plethora of dots and dashes that littered the microfilm. "I suppose you've got some of your savant-minded cronies back at headquarters working on it as we speak, eh, Stone?"

Stone flatly smiled.

"No mind, they won't find anything. It's a singular code that only myself and that autoerotic freak, Barnes, know how to understand anyway. Oh, by the way, he's dead. So now be a nice boy and hand me a paper and pencil so I can begin," said Youngblood.

"So you don't know where the bodies are?" asked Stone. "You have to figure it out from the microfilm."

"Like I said before, my dear Stone, I had nothing to do with the bodies but if you would kindly hand me some writing utensils and paper, I will soon find out where they are located. Oh, by the way, you wouldn't happen to have my transfer papers handy, would you?"

Chapter 12

Dannemora State Prison –
Warden Hawkins' Office

"It's a contingency agreement," said Youngblood's lawyer, a small man with small hands but a large ego. "Nothing more."

His name was Jonathan Petri and he had represented Youngblood in the past on everything from Peeping Tom stuff to full-blown sexual assaults. Now he sat next to the unrepentant sociopath, pen in hand, and ready to sign the document that would get Youngblood transferred to Lompoc.

The prison's Principal Legal Adviser, a man named Brent Carl Williams, slid the document across the table to Petri.

"Just sign where the red *X* marks the spot," said Williams.

Petri perused the document, a document that he had examined *ad nauseum* before the meeting.

"Something's missing, like your signature," said Petri sarcastically.

"We'll sign as soon as you give us the locations of the bodies," said Williams.

Petri produced a large manila envelope and placed it on the table in front of Youngblood.

"Just so we understand each other, Mr. Williams, if you fuck with us I'll have your law license revoked and I'll have you disbarred."

"Go fuck yourself, Petri," said Williams. "Save your scare tactics for the next time that piece of shit client of yours gets his ass in the ringer."

"Now, boys, lawyers are not supposed to talk like that. Shame on both of you," said Youngblood, a prison smirk on his face, and appearing deep down inside to have enjoyed the banter between the two barristers.

"Maybe we'll just figure out the damn code ourselves," said Williams.

"Sure thing," said Youngblood. "All those dots and dashes on the microfilm, well, first, using Morse code figure out what the message is and then take every other word and add up the number of letters in the word, then multiply that number by seven, and then take the logarithm of the resulting number and then add the square root of infinity to it, and then go fuck yourself, because you'll never figure it out," said Youngblood nonchalantly.

"It's a contingency agreement," said Stone. "Both parties just sign it. If we strike out, the document is worthless on its face. Let's get on with it, shall we?"

Williams grabbed the document and signed it and then pushed it back toward Petri, who in turn slide the manila envelope to Williams. Petri and Youngblood then both signed the document.

"We'll start immediately," said Stone. "The cadaver dogs are ready to be transported to the scene and where exactly is that scene, Mr. Youngblood?" asked Stone.

"Check the latitude and longitude in the envelope, Mr. Stone, and if were you I would set up your staging area near

Vestal. It's about a 15-minute drive from Binghamton. Good hunting, Stone," said Youngblood, easing back in his gray-metallic prison chair as if all of his checkers had been kinged and rested in the back row.

Chapter 13

Lompoc Federal Correctional Institution, Lompoc, California
6 Months Later

"I'm so very happy you could come, Stone. Actually, I'm ecstatic." said Youngblood. "And you've brought such a lovely partner with you, how nice."

"This is Agent Masters," said Stone politely.

"And does Agent Masters have a first name, hmm?" asked Youngblood, the false smile of a sociopath adorning his otherwise stagnant face.

"Call me Shelly," Masters said.

"Now then boys and girls, let's have a nice little chat, shall we?"

"It's your dime, Youngblood," said Stone.

"How preceptive of you, Stone. Now then, if you are both comfortable, shall we discuss where the other bodies are buried?"

Passion and Pain

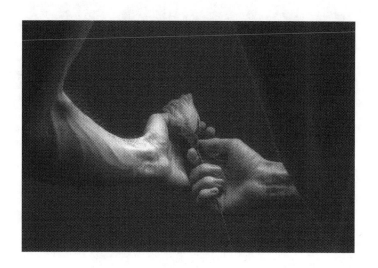

Chapter 1

"It's all about passion," said the Masochist.
"No, it's all about pain," said the Sadist.

Chapter 2

"It's all about pain," said the Masochist.
"No, it's all about passion," said the Sadist.

Chapter 3

It certainly wasn't your typical crime scene, as far as crime scenes go. To describe it as harrowing would be diplomatic. Nonetheless, there it was in colorful photographs spread out on the viewing table in the evidence room in the bowels of the basement where the Special Investigations Unit plied their trade. Investigative Psychologist and retired F.B.I. Agent James Stone, under contract with the Psychological Assessment Unit of the Cook County State's Attorney's Office, sat stoically at one end of the table, while Detective Ronald Raines, a hardened veteran of the Chicago Police Department and stiff-necked witness to many a sordid crime in the City with Big Shoulders, attempted to explain the melee of death that was blanketing the table in an unsavory atmosphere of unexplained evil.

"Ever see anything like it?" asked Raines.

"Only in underground dime novels," said Stone.

"What do you make of it?" asked Raines. "And, better yet, do you think we have a chance with her?"

Make of it? What does one make of unadulterated evil? As far as she was concerned, that would surely be a hard nut to crack.

"We always have a chance," said Stone. "She wants to talk with us. That's a definite start. She's refused legal representation and it's not because of money."

"Right, she's loaded," said Raines.

"It appears that there is an innate need on her part for her to get her story out without someone in the background threading the needle through legal loopholes," said Stone.

"You mean she's somewhat arrogant?" asked Emily Lou Jenkins, a police psychologist also assigned to the Special Investigations Unit, and sitting opposite Raines at the evidence table.

"Arrogant is one thing, Emily," said Stone. "I'd wager that her ego is driving the car and her commonsense is in the backseat."

"A game of sorts?" asked Emily. "Her intellect and view of the world pitted against society's view of right and wrong?"

"Something like that," said Stone. "Now where is she?"

"County brought her over an hour ago. She's upstairs in her nifty orange jumpsuit and her spiffy laceless blue sneakers and manacled to a pole in one of the interview rooms," said Emily.

"Well then, boys and girls, shall we?" asked Stone.

Chapter 4

Her name was as plain as the expression on her adolescent-looking face, Jane Marie Jones. Her hands were neatly folded in front of her as if she were saying her bedtime prayers, one of her dainty wrists manacled to the metal pole that ran from floor to ceiling in the 8 x 8 foot interrogation room with walls colored with dull, gray, chipped paint, and replete with the requisite gun-metal gray table and scratched metal bench of sorrows upon which she sat. If she was 5-feet tall that would be a stretch to the imagination, no pun intended. With her dishpan brown hair tied neatly in a bun, and her face devoid of even a snippet of makeup, she gave Stone the impression of a shy grammar school girl about to enter the classroom on the first day of school. On any other day, at any other time, however, Stone imagined she would have been an acrobat or a gymnast, or even a high-wire daredevil, or with her hair down and flowing across her shoulders, a graceful ballerina dancing to *Swan Lake*. Today, however, she was what she was, a sadistic lust murderer with a penchant for the spectacular all wrapped up into an enigma of which persona she would allow to be unleashed on the skilled interrogators who were presently gazing into her now sterile eyes and searching for a clue, a subtle tell, anything that would give them an advantage in this game of hide and seek on the plain of good and evil in that desolate realm known so well to them all as the Wasteland.

"We have some forms for you to sign before we begin," said Stone, as he seated himself across from her, Raines and Jenkins seating themselves in their respective corners of the room, notepads and pens in hand.

"Forms, of course. Sign my life away, so to speak," she said, a slight glimmer in her eyes, indicating that one of her several personas was about to emerge, that is if she had more than one, thought Stone.

"The first one is Waiver of Counsel. The second one is ..."

"I know what they are, Mr. Stone, and I know who you are. You have quite an impressive biography, if I might say so. Your reputation precedes you. So just push them over to me and I'll sign them and then we can get on with the dissection."

"Dissection?" asked Stone.

"Of whom I am, what I am all about and, of course, the unfortunate incident that has placed me where I am right now," she said, initialing each form with a large black *X*, and then sliding the forms back to Stone.

Stone took the documents, rose from his chair, and then handed them to Raines.

"Just sign in the witness box, Ron, and make a note that she signed with an *X*," said Stone, who then returned to his appointed seat.

"Now then, where shall we begin?" asked Stone. "It is you who have requested this meeting."

"I prefer to call it a conversation," she said, unfolding her hands and massaging her knuckles as if she were expecting a brawl to break out.

"Okay, conversation," said Stone. "You first."

"Shouldn't conversations be private, Mr. Stone? Possibly your cohorts could take a *siesta* in the next room while we continue *our* conversation, hmm?"

Stone expected as much from the hardened sociopath and motioned to the door with a nod of his head as his eyes met his adversary's stare head on. Raines and Jenkins, no amateurs to theatrical manipulation, followed suit and exited the room. Now it was just Stone and a pair of cold and calculating ink-dark eyes born of the Abyss and imprisoned in a young woman's body that gauged each other up and down, as silence became an unwanted interloper in this game of whom would gain the upper hand first.

"I think it's your turn," finally said Stone, breaking the silence.

"There are no turns in conversations, Mr. Stone. Of all people, you should know that. Conversations should simply flow freely between participants, don't you agree?"

"Well, Jane, where would you like to start?" asked Stone.

Her fist from her unshackled hand viscously came down with a reverberating thud on the metal table.

"Don't call me that! *Jane*, how mundane and ordinary. Call me by my dungeon name. That is what we are here to talk about anyway, hmm. Discard *Jane* to the junkyard of your sordid dreams, Mr. Stone. Address me as Mistress Poena."

"And how exactly did you arrive at that moniker?"

"Get out your thesaurus, Mr. Stone. Blood money, penance, punishment, take your pick," she said.

"I was thinking more of pain," said Stone stiffly, as if he had bested her in blackjack, his red ace to her black queen.

"Ah, now you are onto something," she said.

"And what is that?" asked Stone.

"The predecessor or the postscript, depending upon which side of the aisle you have seated yourself."

"The predecessor or the postscript of pain?" asked Stone.

"Why, of course, that is where we should begin. Passion, Mr. Stone. Plain, unadulterated and uncontrollable passion, hmm?"

Chapter 5

"Mistress Poena? How quaint," said Jenkins.

"It means pain or an attribute thereof," said Stone.

"Now that makes sense," said Raines. "Considering that the poor bastard's eyes were sewn shut like a scarecrow's. I suppose she takes pride in her needlework."

"She said it was consensual, consensual rough sex, and simply he got what he wanted. Those were her exact words," said Stone.

"So she admitted to it?" asked Jenkins.

"She does not deny it, Emily. She's hanging her hat, so to speak, on the defense of consensual rough sex. She admits the act but she does not admit the intent to kill. It's an affirmative defense - yes, I did it but …"

"But I whipped him incessantly with a cat-o-nine tails until his back resembled raw strips of bacon and, oh, yes, that was after I had sewn his eyes shut with fishing line. By the way, exsanguination, the cause of death, was not premeditated. Is that about it, Stone?" asked Raines.

"More or less," said Stone.

"Okay, I understand the *less*," said Jenkins. "Now what's the *more*?"

"Well, my gut feeling is that there are more of these so-called consensual sexual encounters that have, shall we say, gone awry, with Mistress Poena acting as the protagonist," said Stone.

"Where?" asked Raines.

"Her activities could have crossed borders," said Stone. "After all, she operated a website, at least that's what she indicated to me."

"Name, please?" asked Jenkins.

"Passion and Pain," said Stone. "I think, Emily, that's under your purview. Please, check it out. Round number two starts tomorrow," said Stone.

"Pain I can understand but what's the passion involved in sewing someone's eyes shut?" asked Emily.

"Depends on which end of the teeter-totter one is sitting," said Stone. "Me, I'm old-fashioned. I don't like pain."

"I vote for passion," said Jenkins.

Raines remained silent, apparently weighing the possibilities.

Chapter 6

It was the same room as before but for some uncanny reason Stone felt confined, as if he were in a convent filled with cloistered nuns. She silently sat across from him with a half-ass smirk on her face, as if to say, *"I told you so."*

"What is it that you told me?" Stone asked.

"You are good at reading people, Mr. Stone. I knew that when I asked to see you but as far as I'm concerned, it's all about tactile response. Are you good at reading braille, Mr. Stone?" she asked, as she spread her hands face-down on the table revealing a planter's field of scar tissue on the top of each hand. "What does this tell you? Touch them if you like, Mr. Stone. Feel the energy. Feel the pain. Feel the passion. Perhaps you can get some psycho-sexual vibes by doing so."

"I'll hold that in abeyance for the time being," said Stone.

"Taking it under advisement, eh, Mr. Stone, how diplomatic of you. Now then where were we from our last meeting?" she asked.

"I think you were going to be more descriptive of what happened," said Stone flatly.

"What happened, my dear Mr. Stone, was consensual rough sex, nothing more. Now then, you do know what a masochist is, don't you, from all of your psychological studies and teaching assignments? At least that's what your resume indicates," she said, easing back a bit into a slumped position.

"A person who derives sexual pleasure from the infliction of pain on himself or herself. It's a sexual perversion," recited Stone.

"Memorized that from your college days, did you? Okay I'll give you a *C-* on that one. But you left out the meat of the answer. It's a person who simply hates himself or herself and their pent-up anxiety is turned inward, which they are afraid to express outwardly as so-called normal individuals do," she said.

"Aggression turned inward toward oneself," said Stone.

"Of course, Mr. Stone, and as the song says, *with a little help from my friends*, and I am that so-called friend."

"So you are the key to the lock, you're the sadist in the equation of innate needs?"

"Well, Mr. Stone, sadism is simply a sexual perversion in which one derives sexual excitement and gratification from the infliction of pain and humiliation upon another, typically leading to orgasm. That's the high-school definition by the way," she said.

"So what's your definition?" asked Stone.

"I'm just a businesswoman, nothing more, nothing less, Mr. Stone. They pay me to wear what they want me to wear. They pay me to do what they want me to do and I do it for an arranged fee. If I derive pleasure or orgasm from it, so be it. That's my little secret. You see, Mr. Stone, my personality lies on the spectrum of sadomasochism, if you really want to know, the simultaneous existence of both submissive and aggressive attitudes in my social and sexual interactions with others," she said.

"But you left out the destructiveness aspect," said Stone.

"That is simply up to them, Mr. Stone. I give them what they pay me to do," she said.

"I'm referring to yourself, to your personality. These little affairs of yours, these business arrangements, so to speak, well, they must certainly lead to a certain degree of disintegration, destructiveness, of whom you really are," said Stone.

"Mr. Stone, you'll never know who I really am. You might understand the *pain* part but you'll never fathom the *passion* part. Now be a nice boy, please, and move to the back of the classroom, hmm, and call the guard. We're through here with this pedantic diatribe," she said, receding into a fetal position and, for all intents and purposes, shutting out the world.

Chapter 7

6 Months Later

James Stone, retired F.B.I. Agent and Investigative Psychologist presently on hiatus from the squalid dregs of murder and mayhem with which he was intimately familiar, took a slow sip of his margarita and then casually opened the e-mail on his cell phone. He was seated in a deck chair on the promenade deck of the luxury cruise ship, near the stern, an island unto himself, as the soft sea breeze wafted across his open shirt.

James: You were correct as usual. She obtained private legal counsel and worked out a plea deal with the prosecutor's office. There was no trial, as you succinctly predicted in your psychological assessment. Her plea was to a lesser charge of Reckless Endangerment, for which she received probation. Again you were spot-on when you predicted that it would be impossible to prove intent, premeditation, with respect to the Capital Murder Offense. The only fly in the ointment, and there always is one, is if she will reoffend again. You predicted that she will and I am with you on that count. Time will only tell. So, wishing you a nice respite from the residue of evil and hope to work with you again in the future. Emily.

Stone closed the e-mail and set the cell phone down next to his margarita. His thoughts wandered in several different directions before being interrupted by a middle-aged and attractive waitress, who was wearing a slim-fitting, one-piece bathing suit, fuchsia in color.

"And what is the gentleman drinking?" she asked, a curious smile on her face.

"Ah, a margarita, and it was quite tasty," said Stone, indicating his drink.

"Well, I have a suggestion for you. Something a little different, perhaps. It has tequila in it and a shot or two of our mystery liqueur. Would you like to try it? It is quite, as you say, tasty."

Her nametag read Abbey and was positioned perfectly on her swimsuit accentuating her cleavage. Why not, thought Stone.

"Okay, I'll give it a try. What's it called?"

She lifted up the drink placard that was on her tray.

"This one," she said, as she pointed it out.

"Hmm, *Passion and Pain*," read Stone out loud. "Sounds luscious."

Chapter 8

Somewhere, Someplace, at Some Unknown Future Time

"Hurt me," said Detective Ronald Raines.

"With pleasure," said Mistress Poena, a glimmer of passion birthing in her otherwise stillborn and sterile eyes, her shiny, black riding crop, form-fitted, with a tapered handle held in one hand, and her low-cut, black latex, one-piece jumpsuit hugging her body as if painted on.

Addendum

Nothing in the Wasteland is simple. Complexities always seem to sprout up out of nowhere when one least expects it. Case in point is one Detective Ronald Raines, a hardened soldier in the war on crime who appears to have witnessed one too many unsavory event in the cesspool of human degradation during his illustrious crime-fighting career. Presently, he has turned that pent-up aggression inward and is teetering on the edge of the Abyss between heaven and hell and waiting for the lash to fall. His succor is pain; his adversary's motivation is bent on passion, as he awaits his self-induced fate.

Ah, but what of his adversary, Mistress Poena, harbinger of misery and disgust, you ask? The simple fact is she will never change, as the esteemed Mr. Stone had clearly indicated in his psychological assessment of her – *once a sociopath, always a sociopath*; and, one would imagine that her business card continues to read: *Passion and Pain –Have Riding Crop, Will Travel.*

As far as our illustrious Mr. Stone, renowned Investigative Psychologist and retired F.B.I Agent, is concerned, one would imagine that he is presently relaxing on the promenade deck of a luxury liner and sipping a margarita knock-off known by the moniker *Passion and Pain*; and, hopefully, after imbibing a few of these concoctions he will be feeling no pain because, if you remember, he's old-fashioned. The other side of the coin, however, involves factoring passion into the equation. Well, reducing that variable can be succinctly satisfied by a middle-aged cocktail waitress named Miss Abbey, who was looking quite engaging and flirtatious in her one-piece, tight-fitting bathing suit, with a plethora of possibilities waiting in the wings. *Voila*!

The Plain Green Book

Chapter 1

Why he had purchased the book he really didn't know. It had an ugly, plain cover resembling pea green soup. It was devoid of lettering and looked like someone's old diary. It was cloth-bound and worn and frayed at the edges and was the size of an ordinary textbook one would typically find in a ceramics class but when he touched it, the cover was smooth and soothing in an antiquarian sort of way. After all, that's what he was – an antiquarian.

Chapter 2

"It dates back to the ancient Egyptians," the antiquarian said. "They had an uncanny proclivity to worship bees."

The man reached out to touch the gold rectangular plaque that was precariously positioned upon the long wooden table in front of him, along with a spattering of several other Egyptian artifacts, but the antiquarian's subsequent reach interceded.

"Ah, but, sir, that is a quite rare and, if I might say so, a rather expensive piece. I would think twice before you touched it."

The man harrumphed a muffled blasphemy between his clenched lips and his overflowing rust-colored moustache.

"Very well, have it your way. How much?"

The antiquarian, a particularly short man with a long neck and drooping ears, perked up his bushy eyebrows.

"Well, sir, as you can see this piece is solid gold. And the ornate depiction of the goddess, who is winged and half-bee, is quite unique. And there is no doubt that she is Egyptian, judging from her headdress. So I would venture to say ..."

"For heaven's sake, Jacob, how much?"

"Well, since you are my half-brother I will certainly concede to your wishes and offer you a price that the gods would assuredly deem generous."

"Enough of your procrastination, I'll give you twenty-thousand. I'm familiar with pieces like this. I have seen them before at bazaars and clearing houses and I know what they are worth."

"But you don't have this one," said Jacob, a slight grin forming at the edges of his small mouth. "Twenty-five."

The man looked around the antiquarian's small shop. It was poorly lit and appeared to not have been swept up for quite some time. He looked down at his shoes, and noticed that they were somewhat covered in dust. And then when he looked up he noticed a stack of books on the counter behind where the haggling over a golden goddess resembling a honeybee had been taking place. The book on the top of the pile for some odd reason caught his fancy. Perhaps it was the pea-green color of the cover, but regardless of that fact, the size was just about right, and he did need a new book that looked like a diary in which to enter his purchases at curious shops like this one.

"Throw in that damn book over there, the one that looked like somebody vomited green pea soup all over it, and we have a bargain."

Jacob looked at the pile of books. Since he had purchased the book, mostly just as a decorative object to take up space in his shop, he really hadn't looked inside of it.

"I just bought it yesterday, just as a curio piece, a simple item that might catch one's attention and it seems to have caught yours. I don't even know what's in it."

"Damn it, do we have a bargain or not?"

And so the bargain had been struck and with the check duly made out, and with the two newly bought items sequestered in separate boxes, Sir Arthur Tractman, descendant of English shepherds, and recent winner of the King's lottery, and subsequent anointed knight, based not upon good deeds, but based simply upon mere donations to certain political campaigns, gleefully skipped out of his half-brother's shop of forgotten curiosities.

Chapter 3

The golden plaque depicting an Egyptian half-bee goddess had found a new home. It had been placed above Sir Arthur's fireplace in his quaint sitting room, which overflowed with oodles of books, one of which, the plain green book, had been relegated to a cluttered and indistinct corner, upon which it sat unopened and resting on a stack of old encyclopedias Sir Arthur had been collecting.

"It is a quite an interesting piece," she said. "I do hope you can part with it."

She was a tall and slender woman with a face that could only be described as inordinately English but her ingrown homeliness was somewhat offset by her quaint smile.

"Part with it? I just obtained it yesterday from my half-brother."

"He's a collector too?"

"An antiquarian in the business of simply making money, if that's what you mean by a collector."

She cinched up her velvet blouse as if she were about to cough, and then gathered herself and sneezed as eloquently as a queen in the parlor eating jam and honey.

"You know there is a certain mystery about a piece like that," she said, somewhat red-faced.

"In what way, Abigail?"

"Well, the Egyptians worshiped the bee as a sacred insect and by incorporating the bee's body as the lower body of an Egyptian woman, well, *voila*, we have a goddess."

"And what is the purpose of this so-called goddess?"

"Myth has it that the goddess is a conduit between Upper and Lower Egypt, between the world as we know it and the underworld."

"Underworld? You mean by rubbing it like Aladdin's lamp one can conjure up evil spirits, ghosts, and zombies? How curious, if I do say so myself."

"Since you are not parting with it, perhaps you should investigate the matter a little further. The goddess Thrai from Comris in Rhodes may be a starting place, as far as the mythology of bees is concerned, somewhere around the 7th century, if my memory serves me well."

"Hmmm," harrumphed Sir Arthur. "Bees, what nonsense."

Abigail turned and was about to leave when she spied the plain green book.

"What an ugly color. It looks like spilled pea green soup. You should burn it. Perhaps that goddess we have been talking about can resurrect some heat and flames from the netherworld and be rid of it. Good day and don't hesitate to call if you change your mind," she said, leaving her calling card on the table.

Chapter 4

He often wondered from where the little red spiders came. They mysteriously appeared every time he sat down at his patio to recollect the events of the day and today was a very pleasant day, and his thoughts were appropriately satisfying, as the little red spiders whisked across the pea green cover of the plain green book, in which he intended to begin writing his memoirs. Memoirs – really recollections of the day's events in the life of a simple, 60-year old, retired English bureaucrat.

One of the tiny red beasts was now crawling up his arm. He wiped it off with the brush of his hand, smashing it to bits and but in doing so, it left a hideous red streak across his arm. He then started to think about colors, the deep red color of the spider and then the ugly pea green soup color of the cover of the book in which he was about to record the day's events. He picked up the book and regarded it at eye-level. Why he kept calling it a book he couldn't quite fathom. Really, it was like an accountant's ledger and just something in which to record tabulations. From where did it come? What was its purpose? Oh, hell with it all. He opened it to the first page. He ran his hand across the empty page. It was rather smooth to the touch and he felt a small flow of electricity enter his fingers. Jut an old book generating a static pulse from non-use, he thought. Kind of like friction maybe. Oh, well, he closed the book and decided on a tall whiskey and soda before he'd begin to recount the day's happenings. He set the book down on the small table next to his reading chair and made his way to the wet bar in the main room as, unknown to him, several small red spiders began crawling across its cover.

Chapter 5

"Odd, isn't it?" said the taller police inspector of the two.

"Quite," responded his partner, a rather slender bloke with an uppity sneer on his face, as if he'd just smelled rotten meat.

"The housekeeper found him there this morning with that book with the ugly green cover nestled on his lap and, according to her, his face rather half-eaten away by a bevy of little red spiders that were still milling around in the area. Damndest thing I ever saw," said the first inspector, his red-brown moustache twisted in a rather precarious way, as if he had slept funny on it the night before.

"Killed by spiders, put that in your next book on murder and mayhem and death investigations," laughed the second inspector.

"Do we need this?" asked the evidence technician, holding up the plain green book and then sweeping away several of the remaining tiny red beasts with his evidence gloves, which he had removed from his hands.

"Nah," said the second inspector. "Allergic reaction most probably to spider bites. Case closed, accidental death."

Chapter 6

He had a habit of keeping everything from crime scenes that nobody wanted. He kept most of the stuff in a back bedroom that he had converted into a storage area. It was getting quite crowded these days but one simple and singular plain green book really wouldn't make much of a difference, especially when it was connected to a rather curious death. As an evidence technician for the Royal Constabulary in London for the past twenty years he had been witness to many a bizarre and unexplained series of deaths, but this one involving the plain green book had really captured his attention. So he placed it on top of a file cabinet chocked full of crime scene photos and other assorted nefarious paraphernalia for the time being, until he could catalogue it and find a final resting place for it. He then checked his watch. His on-and-off fiance, Marsha, would be arriving shortly. So he closed the door behind him, deciding to take a short catnap before she arrived. It wasn't long before he was roused from his sleep. She had let herself in, having a key to his apartment, and now she was whispering in his ear.

"Wake up, Steven. I'm here," Marsha said, as she playfully kissed him on the cheek.

She then placed the small wooden box on the table next to his chair and then smiled, as if she had solved the riddle of the cosmos.

"I take it you have been successful," said Stephen, detecting an emerging glimmer in her eyes.

"Well, it isn't much but it is quite old," Marsha said, indicating the box. "Most probably dating back to prehistoric times and found predominantly in Western Europe. It may be worth something. It may not. It is simply a shard of rock that was probably chipped off of a larger rock, a monolith, if you will."

"But you are in expert in such things, being a Professor of Medieval Antiquities," he said, opening the box and gazing at the jagged shard of gray-white stone.

"Yes, I dare say it is from a menhir or orthostat, a manmade large stone from the Bronze Age found predominantly in Western Europe, and most probably present day France, somewhere around Marseilles. Oh, yes, I would definitely keep it but value-wise, I suppose there is a buyer for everything these days," she said. "Now where shall I put it?"

"Oh, just place it on the black file cabinet next to the green book. I'll get to it in the morning."

With that said, Marsha opened the door to the back bedroom, with which she was intimately familiar, spied the plain green book on top of the file cabinet and placed the small wooden box next to it.

"Such an ugly color. It reminds me of vomited-up pea green soup. What is its significance if any?" she asked, closing the door behind her.

"It was involved in an unexplained death the other day. The victim, so to speak, had his face eaten away by little red spiders while he was holding it. Coincidence or no coincidence, that's what happened," said Stephen. "The inspectors decided it was an accidental death, so they did not need it as evidence."

"And you took possession of it, as is your custom?" she asked.

Stephen only smiled, tapping his fingers on the small table next to where he sat.

"Spiders? Now that's curious in and of itself," said Marsha.

"How so?" asked Stephen.

"Well, was there a spider web involved?" she asked.

"Not exactly. At least I did not notice one."

"Well, if there was one, the spider's web is equated with the concept of fabric. It has a spiral shape and embraces the idea of creation, kind of like being a wheel, everything emanating from its center. But death and destruction often lurk at its center, with the spider smack-dab in the middle. It can symbolize what *Medusa the Gorgon* espoused when placed in the center of certain mosaics."

"And what is that?" asked Stephen.

""Well, a consuming conundrum, a whirlwind of evil, if you will," said Marsha.

"You mean it's a death machine?" asked Stephen.

"I mean it symbolizes the negative aspect of our universe. It is evil personified, at least as far as the Gnostic view is concerned. This is evil at the center, not on the periphery. It is, in essence, the origin of evil."

"So what should I do with it?"

"I would burn it if I were you," she said.

"Burn it?"

"It is like a wheel, a wheel of transformations. Whoever comes in contact with it is transformed in some way."

"Like having their face eaten away by little red spiders?"

"Exactly. So burn it. That's my recommendation."

Chapter 7

Marsha was concerned. Steven called her every morning at 7:00 a.m. promptly. It was now 8:00 a.m. and he had not called. Something was wrong. Perhaps he had fallen. He did have a tendency to have one too many whiskey and sodas on occasion. Now she would have to go over to his apartment and check on him. She looked at her watch again. Not good. He should have called.

When she arrived at his apartment a rather large and burly constable, baton in hand, was standing guard at the door. She read the expression on his face as something untoward had happened inside.

"Not so fast, ma'am," he said. "Police business."

"I'm his girlfriend," said Marsha, the wrinkles under her eyes constricting. "Is he all right?"

Before the constable could answer, a large-framed police detective opened the door.

"You said you are his girlfriend?" he asked. "I'm Detective Workman."

He appeared to be in his late 50's with sparkling gray hair and a neatly trimmed matching moustache. His bulky frame dwarfed the entrance to the door and she could not see inside.

"Yes, Detective, please, is he okay?"

"Well, ma'am, it appears to have been an accident. Please, follow me," he said.

Steven was sprawled out on the floor half in and half out of the entrance to the back bedroom. He was lying on his back with the shard of prehistoric rock lodged deeply in his forehead between his eyes. The plain and ugly pea green soup-colored book was clutched in one of his hands. The expression on his face was flat, as if he had died an instant death.

"Seemed to have fallen and somehow or other that jagged piece of stone found an unfortunate resting place between his eyes. I imagine he died an abrupt and instant death. That whiskey tumbler on the floor beside him, I think, is the culprit," said the detective. "Did he have a tendency to over-imbibe, ma'am, if I may cut to the chase?"

Marsha was listening but taking in the awful scene had somewhat muted what the good detective had been asking. Refocusing, she responded to his questions.

"Yes, yes, he was a whiskey and soda man on a nightly basis but nothing like this had ever happened before. I was here just yesterday and both of those items were on top of the file cabinet," she said, indicating the three-drawer, black file cabinet found in the typical barrister's office.

"Well, then, seemed he was reaching for them, the items I mean, and, well, too many whiskies and sodas can off-set one's equilibrium and balance, if you know what I mean, ma'am."

"Tripped and fell and that jagged shard of stone killed him, is that what you mean?"

"Accidental death, plain and simple, ma'am," said the Detective. "Now then, is there a next of kin or …"

"No, no, no, just me. There should be a will around here somewhere. I'm named as the executor," said Marsha, stifling back the tears.

"Well, then it appears all this stuff in there will be under your provenance," said the detective indicating the back bedroom.

"You'll not need any of it for your investigation?" Marsha asked.

"No, ma'am, accidental death, plain and simple."

"*Medusa the Gorgon*," she whispered under her breath.

"What did you say?" asked Detective Workman.

"Oh, nothing, just thinking out loud," she said.

Chapter 8

"*Medusa the Gorgon*," Marsha said.

"What?" asked Francine.

"It's Greek mythology," said Marsha.

"I'm just a hairdresser, you know that. You're the expert in those other things," said Francine. "Now tell me exactly what you think killed him," said Francine.

"It was not an accident. That's for sure, Francine. It was something else," said Marsha, wringing her hands as if she had uttered a blasphemy.

"Something else? You mean someone else?" asked Francine.

"Something," Marsha whispered.

"What did you do with the book?" asked Francine. "I hope you burned it."

"I took it home and put it in the wall safe in my bedroom."

"What in God's name for? Way up there behind the picture with the flowers? You'll need a step ladder to get to it," said Francine.

"Exactly. It's in a safe place where no one can get to it and, conversely, it can't get to anyone else until I figure out what happened," she said.

"Well, what's in it? What's it all about?" asked Marsha.

"To tell you the truth, Francine, I never looked inside of it."

Silence filled the room like cyanide gas entering a gas chamber as two sets of eyes met each other on the edge of the Abyss, while the decision to enter the Gates of Hell held center stage.

"Maybe we should take a look," said Francine. "Just to be safe."

"Okay," said Marsha. "I'll sleep on it."

"Tomorrow?" asked Francine.

But Marsha wasn't listening. She was thinking about the plain green book and if it did, in fact, have a life of its own.

Chapter 9

Francine was terrified when she first saw them, the three Gorgons about which Marsha had warned her. She closed her laptop after having Googled *Medusa the Gorgon*. How could they be connected to that simple plain green book that Marsha feared they had somehow infected? How ridiculous. This was the 21st century and they were from Greek mythology, of all places. The more she thought about it, the more she could not get the monstrous images out of her mind. Medusa, who was referred to as Gorgo, was depicted as a winged human female having living and writhing venomous serpents in place of hair. It was believed that anyone who gazed into her eyes would turn to stone. There were two other Gorgons described, as well, but for some odd reason Francine had become fixated on Medusa. Perhaps it was because she was so beautiful. No wonder stranded sailors would look into her eyes and then, of course, turn to stone. There was a certain hatred of human mankind imbued in her image.

Francine, a hairdresser by trade, began to fantasize about what it would be like servicing Medusa, a beautiful woman with poisonous serpents for hair. Where would she even begin? She laughed to herself, how insanely ridiculous. She turned off the light and got into bed. Soon she was entering that twilight realm where images fluttered about with no exact purpose. As she began to enter deep sleep, images of the Gorgons appeared.

Chapter 10

3 Days Later

"A neighbor found them," said the first inspector, a rather stout man with large feet and large hands and who was addressed as Inspector Rinbaugh.

"Seems to be the thing these days," said the second inspector who was tall, slender and wiry in appearance, and whose name was Inspector Bancock.

"The outer door was open and, well, take a look for yourself," said Inspector Rinbaugh.

Inspector Bancock approached the two women who were sprawled on the floor in the bedroom, a rather tall step ladder impinging on the skull of the shorter of the two, dried rivulets of copper-colored blood making a trail almost to the entranceway of the bedroom.

"Skull's smashed in pretty good," said Inspector Bancock.

"Heavy ladders can do that," said Inspector Rinbaugh.

"And the second victim, your thoughts?" asked Inspector Bancock.

"Climbing the ladder, no doubt, to get to that wall safe that's open."

"Lost her balance and fell off the damn thing, did she?"

"Appears so and right on top of the other woman who apparently was holding the ladder. Crushed her skull pretty good, too."

The death scene was cordoned off with red tape. Inspector Rinbaugh deftly maneuvered over it and picked up the plain green book that lay opposite of the melee of death.

"Appears one of them removed this from the wall safe and then all hell broke loose," said Inspector Rinbaugh.

"All this carnage for a damn book, and an ugly one at that. Looks like some drunken bloke spewed chewed-up asparagus all over it."

Inspector Rinbaugh chuckled and then set the plain green book on the lone coffee table in the room.

"Won't be needing that and neither will they," said Inspector Rinbaugh.

"Accidental deaths, plain and simple," said Inspector Bancock, as the evidence technicians continued to minister to the two unfortunate victims of yet another unsavory episode of the plain green book.

Addendum

How the plain green book found its way to its present resting place is only conjecture. Its current home was a quaint curio shop located in Surrey, England located near the border with greater London on the northeast. The shop was not a bookshop, *per se*, but dabbled in many items of which the typical tourist would find interesting.

It was on a late autumnal day, the wind brisk, and the skies a cloudy London gray, that a family of three visiting nearby castles in the area stumbled into the shop. The young wife was quickly attracted to a bevy of sparkling earrings that hung on a manikin in one corner of the shop, while the young husband meandered about the section in which ornamental armor and pictures of jousting events were displayed. The young boy approaching his 9th birthday disappeared into the bowels of the shop unnoticed.

Window shopping and shopping in general typically result in time being lost in the bucket of non-factors, and so it was here, in this small curio shop on the border with London proper that after several hours of perusing the curious items on display that a sparkling pair of onyx earrings was purchased for the young wife, and a portrait of a jousting event held in the court of Henry the VIII was obtained after a bit of haggling with the proprietor for the young husband.

The young boy was not to be outdone. He emerged from the shadows of the rear of the shop, the plain green book in one hand, and an assortment of colored pencils in the other.

"Father," he said, "May I?"

The plain green book and the colored pencils were extended outward by anxious and imploring hands, succinctly followed by a nod and a smile by the young father.

"It's a book, Jason," said the young wife. "How will you color in it?"

"It is empty, mother, take a look," he said.

The young mother took the book and began paging through it.

"Well, Jason, you are right and you are wrong. Please, look on the last page," she said.

Jason took back the book and flipped to the end. The last page of the book contained a table of contents. Chapter 1 read *Little Red Ants*. Chapter 2 read *Monoliths*. Chapter 3 read *Medussa the Gorgon*. Chapter 4 was blank.

"Well," said Jason. "I think I can come up with something for Chapter 4. I can certainly color little red ants and a monolith is nothing more than a big stone. We learned that in history class."

"Very well," said the young father. "How much?"

"Oh, take it as a gift," said the proprietor. "Seeing that you both have made significant purchases."

"Thank you very much," said the young mother.

As they were leaving the shop, Jason, turned towards his parents.

"What's a gorgon?" he asked.

The Woman Who Lived Upstairs

Chapter 1

You could spot her from a mile away and you could smell her from two. Her dress fit tightly, what there was of it, and she was all legs, the kind of legs that could twist a man's mind into mush and make him want to watch Oprah over and over again. Yes, Miss Scarlet Marie Burns was all legs but she was all lies, too, and that's what made it interesting; fishing out the truth from a cesspool of conjecture, innuendo and outright fabrication. Yes, Miss Scarlet, as I came to call her, was an expert at deception and spellbinding incantations of bullshit mixed in with a subtle truth here and there and if she did anything, she brought out the detective in me. That's my job, anyway, sorting out the bullshit. Oh, by the way, I'm Detective Frank Peron, Robbery-Homicide, Chicago Police Department, and she, well, let's just say she was the woman who lived upstairs.

Chapter 2

The old cup of sugar trick went out in the '50's, along with peach pies cooling on windowsills while *Summer Wind* by Frank Sinatra was playing on the radio, along with TVs without clickers. So Miss Scarlet had to improvise and think of something else. This time it was something that women generally had no clue about, a running toilet. So that's how Miss Scarlet came to knock on my door one frigid night in mid-December, imploring me in her not so innocent way to help her out, so to speak. It really was simple, the toilet, I mean. Just an adjustment of the chain on the plunger and the running stopped and there we stood in her apartment on the floor just above mine staring at each other as I was getting ready to leave.

"Thank you again, Mr. Peron," she said, smiling and extending her hand, a soft hand bejeweled with a ring on each finger and as white as snow, and smelling of sweet rose oil.

I gently shook it with my good hand, a custom I find inconvenient. Shaking hands with women always makes me nervous but not as nervous as dealing with women with hyphenated names. Miss Scarlet's name, however, was straightforward and succinct, just as her appearance and demeanor seemed to be. Ah, yes, Miss Scarlet, at least that's what she told me she preferred to be called, and that's what

I did end up calling her, at least in the beginning, but after that, well, I called her many things, some of them not so pleasant. But I'm getting way ahead of myself. Back to Miss Scarlet, the running toilet, and the handshake that was, well, anticipated, inconvenient, and yet inviting. I thought about it for a moment; yes, future clandestine relations in cozy, romantic locations, with soft music playing, and with lots and lots of hot, uninterrupted, decadent sex appeared to be on the horizon. Well, I was partly right and partly wrong and that, dear reader, led to a plethora of dilemmas and unexpected outcomes of which I am about to tell you.

But on that night of first encounters appearances were extremely important and her shorter-than-short miniskirt, blood-red in color, and revealing those slender twin sentinels of delight, was on what I was focused. Maybe I should have spent more time figuring out her nonverbal cues. After all, I was a detective, as opposed to lusting after her feminine anatomy but unfortunately for me, being a steadfast member of the police subculture, I succumbed to the latter and not to the former. So when it came right down to it, it was all about the leg show that evening.

"I really didn't mean to impose on you," she had said, pouty lips melding with the slow batting of sensuous eyelashes. "Especially when your arm is in a sling."

Yes, I was recovering from a particularly bad injury suffered while executing a no-knock search warrant in the middle of the night on a supposed meth lab. Suffice it to say, being the first one through the door after the battering ram had rent its fury can be somewhat problematic and on that particular occasion a 2 x 4, about six feet long and waterlogged, had been viciously wielded by a heavyset and dimwitted lookout guarding the lab. It had struck me flush on the back of my left shoulder. The result, of course, was unpleasant and the two surgeries that followed, including the second one where a metal plate was inserted onto my upper humerus with the corresponding fourteen screws, you see it was a compound fracture, were even more unpleasant. So with my metal-laden left arm neatly secured in a sling, my talking was assisted with only the use of my good hand. I have a tendency to talk with both of my hands anyway, probably due to the fact that my mother was a full-blooded Italian and only stood about five feet tall.

"Oh, that. It's not as bad as it looks," I lied, the dull throb and shooting pains unrelenting in my upper arm and making me want to jump out of my foreskin.

"Did you hurt it on the job? The landlord said that you are a detective."

"Yes, on the job, executing a drug warrant," I said, readjusting the sling to a more or less comfortable position, mostly less.

"Well, if you ever need someone to massage it for you, it's the least I could do. So don't be a stranger. Call me anytime," she winked, eyes twinkling, deep violet, mysterious and inviting.

Massage *it*. I thought she was referring to my arm but her eyes were riveted elsewhere, somewhere south of the border down Mexico way. She then grabbed a small pad of paper from a nearby coffee table and scribbled her phone number on it.

"Here, this is my cell number and thanks so much, Detective," she said, a feline smile forming on her imploring lips.

And that was my first encounter with Miss Scarlet and her legs of a thousand mysteries. The rest is history but what an unpleasant history it turned out to be.

Chapter 3

Convalescent leave can be good or bad. For guys with hobbies like stamp collecting and playing bingo it was always good, just ask Curly. By the way that would be Woodrow Curly Evans. No one called him Woodrow unless they wanted their ass summarily kicked. So all of us homicide dicks called him Curly, even though he was as bald as an eight ball. Curly was a good cop and played bingo incessantly, a ten-card kind of guy on a bad night, but if he was winning the sky was the limit. Anyway, after getting shot a couple of times in the leg the limp just wouldn't go away, so good old Curly found himself in the bingo hall most nights and loved it. Disability leave worked wonders for him but for me, bereft of even an inkling of a hobby or avocation, nursing my mangled arm back to health was sheer boredom, but then Miss Scarlet entered the picture and everything changed.

The phone rang the morning after the toilet escapade. I usually get up at the crack of dawn anyway, an old habit I had acquired from working homicide cases; biological clocks and circadian rhythms can be so annoying at times. It was Miss Scarlet again and so I set my cup of coffee down and placed my cell phone on speaker. A sling in one arm was really causing me to adjust my life mechanics. So with my good hand secured around the hot cup of liquid black tar that was pretending to be coffee, I listened to the sensuous voice from upstairs.

"Sorry to bother you again, Frank, or should I call you Detective, but if you're up, I hope I haven't disturbed you, have I?" she asked.

"Frank will do just fine," I replied, my 6th cop sense getting revved up.

I pictured her sitting in front of the mirror, legs slightly spread, wearing a see-through black negligee and putting red lipstick on her somewhat botoxed lips and in between the puckering and lip smacking her words flowed out, as if released slowly from a starter's pistol.

"I was hesitant to bother you but …"

"No, just having a cup of coffee. Well, I think it's coffee anyway. I get up early these days," I said, interrupting her.

"Oh, good, I would hate to be an inconvenience."

An *inconvenience*? The only inconvenience I could think of was her removing her cheetah-like legs from around my face after she had removed her flowered panties, but that simple feat had yet to transpire. Oh, well, give it time. Let's see what the denizen from the dungeon of feminine delights wants now.

"Oh, no, not at all. You know, I'm just pondering whether any of those objects in the Kuiper Belt will ever make it to earth," I said.

"Oh, Frank, c'mon, don't worry about your waist line. It's just fine."

Chalk up astronomy as something Miss Scarlet missed out on.

"Ah, yeah, you're right. So what can I do for you, fix your toilet again, lend you a million bucks, give you the best back massage you've ever had in your life?"

"You're funny but what I really need is a ride downtown later, around noon that is, if you're up to it."

I looked out of the window. My car was buried under a sheet of ice, snowflakes as big as flapjacks were beginning to fall, and my arm was throbbing to the beat of *The William Tell Overture,* but miss out on a ride downtown with Miss Scarlet and her legs of a thousand intrigues, no way, Jose.

"Just call me when you're ready. I'll be up and about in a jiffy," I said.

"Oh, you're such a darling. I knew I could count on you. About noon then," she said, as the line went dead.

I looked at my watch. Then I looked outside. Mercy, better get out the snow shovel and start digging out my car with my good arm but before I could cinch up my boxers she was on the line again and crying hysterically.

Chapter 4

The first time I kissed her, her lips tasted of bourbon and honey, as if she had been drowning her sorrows and drinking all night. Yet her skin was smooth and delicate, as if she had rubbed olive oil all over it. It hadn't been but a moment or two after I had entered her apartment that she had wildly flung herself into my arms. Her kisses were passionate and flowed evenly across my face, as her tears subsided and as she began whispering in my ear. It was all I could do to restrain myself from losing my composure but then again it was all so sudden. Women have that special knack of uncannily placing a guy off-guard, especially attractive women with long slender legs and who could whisper like Mata Hari.

"You're not Dutch, are you?" I asked her.

"Heaven's no," she said catching her breath. "Is this another one of your funny cop jokes, Frank? If it is, I can be Dutch if you want me to be."

She was smiling as she continued to peck at my neck.

So much for the exotic dancer and courtesan angle.

"So what is your nationality?" I asked her, as the pecking increased to the speed of sound.

"I'm from Tennessee," she said with a sensuous drawl that could have been birthed from anywhere below the Mason-Dixon line.

So much for genealogy.

"I see," I said. "A southern lady."

"Well, I'm glad that you consider me a lady. That deadbeat of an ex-husband surely doesn't."

"Is that why you were crying? Is that why I'm here?" I asked her.

"You are a detective, aren't you?" she coyly asked, her lips all over my face and the way they were zigging and zagging one would have needed GPS to determine where they were headed next.

I couldn't respond, however, because my tongue was tied in somewhat of a Gordian Knot with hers and then she released me. While I was regaining what composure I had left and attempting to ascertain what her true agenda was, she put her slender finger across my lips and in her southern drawl she whispered in only the way that true courtesans and exotic dancers could.

"Have you ever been to Tennessee?" she asked.

Chapter 5

Somehow I was convinced that somewhere in her past she had been both a courtesan and an exotic dancer, and most probably in Tennessee. Whether or not she was Dutch, like Mata Hari had been, remained to be seen. So when you factored Tennessee into the mix of things, well, maybe that's where bourbon, her apparent choice of intoxicants, entered the picture.

There was really no trip to be made downtown, as she had requested my help in accomplishing. It was just one of her simple ploys she typically used to, more or less, get her way and her way at this moment in time was travelling to her birthplace in Tennessee to, as she had said, check on some deeds to various properties that her ex-husband was attempting to swindle from her. So we found ourselves travelling in my late model Mercury Marquis, white in color, paid-off, and that took a bump like a Sherman tank. It was an old people's car, no doubt about that but, approaching 50, I really didn't consider myself old but certainly older than Miss Scarlet whom I estimated to be in her early thirties. Our destination was Putnam County Tennessee, the small town of Algood where she had been born and raised, to be specific.

"You know, Frank, I am going to pay you," she said.

"Don't worry about it, Miss Scarlet. This beats sitting around the house and watching Oprah," I said. "Anyway, I'm getting disability pay from the Department."

"Well, after we straighten this thing out about the deeds I'll be coming into a considerable amount of money," she said.

Then she squinted at me in that funny sort of way that women exhibit when they think they have noticed something odd.

"Is your arm hurting you, Frank? Do you want me to drive?" she asked.

It's difficult to drive when one of your arms is cinched up in a sling but, no, I didn't want her to drive. As far as my arm hurting me, yes, it was killing me. Maybe she was clairvoyant.

"No, driving's okay but are you telepathic?" I asked with somewhat of a grin on my face.

"No, I'm Presbyterian," she said. "But why do you ask? Is it because you are a Catholic?"

She was right. I am a Catholic or was back in my altar boy days. Maybe she was clairvoyant after all.

"How did you know?" I asked.

"You just have that funny altar boy look on your face like you are suppressing impure thoughts," she said. "You aren't having impure thoughts about me, are you Frank?"

She was leaning back and smiling at me. Maybe leering would be a better description but impure thoughts, well, if fantasizing about Mis Scarlet in red-laced, crotchless panties and wearing matching sequined stiletto heels while doing the Rhumba on my face with the song *All Night Long* by Lionel Ritchie playing softly in the background was fantasizing, well, then she had me on that one.

"Not really," I lied. "Just thinking about the motel tonight. Don't you think we should get separate rooms? I'm quite a thrasher with my arm in a sling. I don't think you'd get much sleep."

"Don't worry about getting any sleep tonight, Frank," she whispered, winking at me and biting her lower lip. "Thrashing in bed is one of my hobbies."

All Night Long started to play in the back of my mind again.

Chapter 6

I'll dispense with a characterization of the nocturnal extracurricular activities that had just taken place between yours truly and Miss Scarlet. Let's just say that, as we entered my car en route to Algood, *All Night Long* continued to play incessantly in the back of my mind.

"What was that tune you were humming most of the night? I just couldn't place it," she asked, seating herself next to me as if we were headed for a drive-in movie.

"Oh, nothing really. I can't carry a tune. I guess I was just caught up in the moment," I said, as *All Night Long* began playing again at high-pitch in the back of my mind.

"Well, that's okay, about humming, I mean. You were good at other things," she said, smacking her lips like a drunken wench on a pirate ship, and then nuzzling closer to me.

Miss Scarlet was good at other things, as well, but I just couldn't figure out where all of this was heading. So I posed the question to her that had been bothering me for quite some time.

"Your ex-husband, is he in Algood?"

"You are so perceptive, Frank," she whispered in my ear.

"I'll take that as yes," I said. "And ..."

"And what?" she sensuously whispered.

I simply looked into her dancing violet eyes in order to determine her demeanor.

"You do know that we have to take care of him, don't you?" she said.

I figured as much but *take care of him*, I would have to Google that to determine exactly what Miss Scarlet had in mind.

"I had an idea something like that was on your mind," I said, as she nuzzled closer to me, began nibbling on my ear, and as *All Night Long* slowly began creeping from my gray matter.

Chapter 7

Algood, Tennessee, well, what can be said about that quaint little burb? Probably that the highlight in town for the average god-fearing and law-abiding citizen was the Tastee-Freeze located smack-dab in the middle of Main Street. For the other inhabitants who were classified more on the flip-side of the coin of morality and decadence, it was the road house located on the outskirts of town that was named *Angie's* and that advertised on a rather large marquis with flickering red and pink lights, *Girls, Girls, Girls.* Somehow or other *deja vu* struck me succinctly between the eyes as we passed that hovel of disgust and intrigue. I imagined that Miss Scarlet and *Angie's* were connected by some kind of a common denominator. What exactly, however, that common denominator was at the moment was merely conjecture. So I posed the question.

"Ever been there?" I asked. *"Angie's?"*

She looked at me somewhat cross-eyed and biting her lower lip as if her undies were too tight and running up the crack of her ass.

"No respectable girl would frequent that establishment, mister. Now keep your eyes on the road," she responded and then quickly looked away from me, her lower lip somewhat quivering.

Well, that about cinched it for me, my cop intuition shifting into high gear. I'd have to mosey on over to *Angie's* later in the day and do a little investigating without *you-know-who* knowing about it, of course. Things were getting more curious by the moment and my cop ears were perking up and checking the radar whenever I thought about Miss Scarlet and her apparent hidden agenda.

Chapter 8

"You a cop or somethin'?" she asked, her mounds of cleavage pouring out of her somewhat nightgown, coverall or coverless, whatever the hell it was.

"What would give you that idea?" I asked. "You must be Angie, I assume."

That brought a twinkle to her eyes; deep glacier blue and seductively imploring in the way of all flesh.

"Well, you are sitting in the back of the bar with your back against the wall, aren't you? Your hands are under the table and probably massaging a sidearm or can of pepper spray. Your hair is short like the way cops wear it and, oh, I do like your silver hair. It reminds me of Kenny Rogers in his heyday, and you have that deep-seated cop look on your face."

"Cop look? Oh, you dated one?"

"Several, mister. Now what is it that you exactly want? If it's a girl, well, if you are off-duty that can be arranged," she said, pulling up a chair and sitting across from me Annie Oakley style while the only things missing were a branding iron and a Winchester repeating rifle.

She was the kind of girl you wouldn't bring home to mother. Now father, that was an altogether different matter. I think it was her pink stiletto heels that matched her lipstick and the flickering lights in the marquis hanging above her

309

cathouse, or perhaps it was the tighter-than-tight, black-laced see-through something-or-other that she was kind of wearing. Anyway, that was my first impression and first impressions are usually right. So, I pulled out my cell phone and dialed up a photo of Miss Scarlet I had recently taken.

"Ever seen her before?" I asked, showing her the photo.

"You're dating yourself, mister, or should I say detective. She hasn't been around here for about a year or so but Tassie over there has a close resemblance to her. Should I fetch her over here for a look-see?"

"Well, yes, detective is more than apropos, Angie, but as far as Tassie, I am not exactly looking for a fling in the hay at the moment. Maybe another time. I'm just trying to gather some background on Miss Scarlet, the woman in the photo."

"Well, then, Tassie's your girl. She's Miss Scarlet's cousin, a little bit more back-woodsy but just as pretty."

Chapter 9

Well, let's cut to the chase, shall we? To say that Tassie was a wealth of information is being downright unflattering. In fact, she put the whole gamut of Miss Scarlet and her somewhat perverted agenda in focus. It was all about money, as it usually is. In this particular case it was about deeds to property where coal veins were discovered, the deeds in question being recorded in the name of her ex-husband. So why was I recruited to accompany her down here to Algood, Tennessee? Well, it appears that some showing of muscle was in the offing and I was that muscle. So what happened next, you ask? Well, here is the long and the short of it.

I had become real curious when Miss Scarlet asked me during a respite from our nocturnal activities the night before if I had brought my shiny police revolver with me. I was somewhat cross-eyed at the time, incessant necking can do that to a guy, and I didn't give it a second thought when I told her that it was in the trunk of my vehicle wrapped in a blanket. How she knew I had a revolver with me and not a pistol, was quite intriguing. So I asked her. "You just look like a wheel gun guy," she had said and I left it at that, as the aforementioned necking increased in intensity.

So after getting the low-down from Miss Tassie about the nefarious agenda of Miss Scarlet, well a short trip to the local general store was in order. There I met, Elmer, the proprietor, showed him my police shield and confided in him that I needed to purchase a box of blank rounds for my revolver, just for shits-and-giggles. Well, suffice it to say six of those blank rounds found a nesting place in my revolver, which was secreted in the trunk of my car. The rest is history, as they say.

Chapter 10

She looked somewhat out of place behind bars. Attempted murder charges can be so annoying! I felt sorry for her in that former girlfriend-boyfriend sort of way but that only lasted for a few seconds, especially when I remembered that she tried to drug me, steal my gun, plant a few rounds in her ex-husband's forehead with my service revolver, replete with my fingerprints all over it, and then blame everything on me. Thanks to Tassie, however, that little so-called escapade of intrigue was nipped in the bud and when the rounds went off, the blanks, if you will, the expression on her face was as blank as the rounds she had just fired at her ex-husband. Then when the handcuffs were placed on her dainty wrists by Deputy Rufus T. Suggs, who just happened to be surveilling the sordid event from an adjacent room, well, any hint of sublime confidence that had been implanted on her face was summarily deposited in the wastebasket of her emotions.

Tassie, I guess it was the Mata Hari in her, the interloper, clandestine spy, quisling, whatever you want to call it, really carried the day. Kissing cousins no more, she had decided to do the right thing after having been taken into confidence by Miss Scarlet and, well, the rest, as they say, is history.

Epilogue

Oh, Tassie, you ask? Well, she certainly had a striking resemblance to Miss Scarlet. That's for sure but, in fact, when I thought about it for any length of time, there appeared to be something uniquely striking about her that attracted me to her. It was her honesty and that, my dear reader, is how I arranged for her to move back to Chicago and away from all of that petty nonsense and inbred squabbling that Algood provided. Although her trade lied in the exotic dancing and courtesan sphere, I found her a job working for the apartment manager in my building that offset her rent and she was quite appreciative. Somehow or other the ex-husband of *you know who* provided her with a deed to a parcel of the coal-infested property that led the unfortunate demise of Miss Scarlet. I think it stemmed from saving his ass from being shot. I, of course, was not interested in remuneration. I only wanted to extricate myself from such an unfortunate and downright annoying situation and get back to the City with Big Shoulders and nurse my ailing arm back to normalcy.

Suffice it to say, that being home in the friendly confines worked wonders for me and my injured arm and, by the way, Tassie was inordinately helpful in nursing me back to health in more ways than one, physically and psychologically. I think it was her resemblance from the waist down to Mata Hari. From the waist up she even had a tinge of the Dutch look to her. I think it was her smile when she was kissing me. Oh, I'd be remiss if I didn't tell you. You see, she moved into Miss Scarlet's old apartment and forever more would be known to me as the woman who *lives* upstairs.

Printed in the United States
by Baker & Taylor Publisher Services